"My Sister – the superbitch"

"Mum, I got drunk – it was an accident! I'll never do it again. But that's all there is to it!"

"Oh, yes? And how exactly do you explain what Faith saw?"

"What Faith saw was Mikey – Mr Kershaw – helping me outside when I felt sick. End of story."

"That's not what Faith says; she says you were kissing and cuddling when she saw you. She—"

"Mum, Faith's a bitch!" I exploded, looking from one face to another – one ashen white, the other stupidly smug. "No, that's not quite right – she's a superbitch! A real champion of bitchiness! Lying, backstabbing – you name it, she's a real expert at it all! In fact—"

"That's enough, Christine! All Faith and I care about is your welfare! A grown man seems to be in danger of taking advantage of you, and she's doing what she thinks is right to stop that from happening."

"My sister - the superbitch"

Rosie Corrigan

SCHOLASTIC

For two sisters who are always super and
never bitches – Claire and Emma McCombie.

Scholastic Children's Books
Commonwealth House, 1–19 New Oxford Street,
London WC1A 1NU, UK
A division of Scholastic Ltd
London ~ New York ~ Toronto ~ Sydney ~ Auckland

First published in the UK by Scholastic Ltd, 1998

Copyright © Rosie Corrigan, 1998

ISBN 0 590 11151 5

Typeset by Falcon Oast Graphic Art
Printed by Cox and Wyman Ltd, Reading, Berks.

10 9 8 7 6 5 4 3 2 1

Prologue

The deal with Rob is that I get to switch rooms with him as long as (a) I do all the shifting round, and (b) I paint over the floral border in my old room. Sleeping in a room that's about as big as the garden shed he can cope with, he says, but flowery décor, no way. That seems pretty fair. I know it's not like he's going to be at home too much anyway (you can't just pop back and forth for the odd weekend all the way from India, can you?), but I don't know if I'd have given up such a brilliant room if it was the other way round.

Laurie's gone now; she had to go home and get ready for the barbecue, but she helped me move everything round really quickly this afternoon. I'm sitting at Rob's huge old wooden desk (my huge old wooden desk?), looking out of the window at our neat little garden, and the mad sprawling jungle that belongs to next door. I swear our cat goes in there and doesn't come out for days.

I spin round on the creaky office chair, pull my knees up to my chin and survey my empire. The futon bed, over to the left by the door, looks different now I've swapped Rob's black cotton duvet cover for my blue checked one. It goes better with the pale blue walls, though. The squidgy sofa that was Gran's is straight in front of me, with a big multicoloured Indian throw chucked over. It just about covers it, but the odd hideous brown and orange swirly corner does tend to reveal itself now and then. On my right is the walnut wardrobe and chest of drawers (both Gran's) with the orange glass handles that used to remind me of sweets when I was little, and the low coffee-table that Rob's old TV and video are plonked on, as well as the CD player. (Yes, I get to keep those too!) Apart from clothes and books and stuff, the only thing I've hauled through from my room is my cheese plant: like me, it was outgrowing the boxroom.

It feels weird having the luxury of free time, now the exams are over. What shall I do next? I've got about an hour to kill before we all go through to the barbecue. I could unpack the cardboard boxes in the middle of the floor, or dig the white paint out of the shed, ready to attack the floral border. For a second or two while I think, I watch the recently unsettled specks of dust drift in the early evening sunlight streaming through the window behind me. No, both of those can wait till tomorrow; right now, I'm going to write a long, *long* letter to Beth. I've been terrible at keeping in touch with her since she moved away. I haven't told her anything about what's been going on these last few months, especially what's happened between me and Faith. That's going to take some telling. . .

"Oi, Conk! Is this yours?" I turn round in time to see Faith disappearing from the doorway as a videotape hurtles towards my head.

It's my long-missing copy of *Friends*, Series one, Volume three. Welcome back!

I thump my A4 pad of paper on the desk, scrabble around for a biro that works, and get ready to spill the many beans that need to be spilled. So at what point should I start? Is there a starting-point? I suppose there is: it was the day Mr Kershaw arrived at school. . .

Chapter 1

It was an average dreary, drizzly March day. And it was your average Monday morning, I guess. The usual kerfuffle was going on downstairs on the bus.

"You can't use that pass yet, love; it's not nine o'clock."

"Oh, it's definitely past nine, dear."

"Look, see all those kids trying to get on behind you? If it's past nine o'clock, then they'd all be late for school and up for detention, right?"

"Well, that's the youth of today for you, son. They just don't care."

"Please just get off the bus and let the other passengers on. . ."

I could hear tonnes of shuffling and groaning going on, as well as the odd "C'mon, grandma!" It was the same every morning: around twenty to nine, there she'd be at the bus-stop, with her tartan shopping trolley, tweed coat and the handful of excuses that she rotated day by day. "Well, *my* watch says nine!", "They said it was nine on the telly, and they can't be wrong, can they?", "I'm eighty-three, you know, and can't see the hands of my watch too clearly" and (my favourite), "Well, you must be driving too fast, young man. You've obviously arrived here too early, and that's not my fault, is it?"

I'd never managed to figure out what an eighty-three-year-old lady had to do so early in the morning that made it worth trying to cheat her way on to the bus. And it wasn't as if any of the drivers ever let her get away with it. I once decided she must be an undercover inspector for the bus company, making sure they were sticking to the rules. Or maybe the excitement of a confrontation gave her a bit of an adrenaline rush for the day. I mean, it's not like you can do too much that's radical and dangerous when you're eighty-three. Riding fast motorbikes and bungee-jumping must be pretty much out when you've got to take your tartan trolley with you everywhere. Whatever her reason, at least it made the bus journey to school that little bit more interesting.

Sitting in my usual front-seat-on-the-top-deck spot this particular morning, I waited for the thundering of feet coming up the stairs, after the old dear finally gave up for the day. I didn't turn round to see who was there, just in case a pair of those stomping size sevens were Faith's. I knew I'd find out soon enough if she'd got on at this stop.

"Yoo hoo! Saddo at the front! Not speaking?" A cackle of giggles erupted from the back of the bus. Here we go, I thought. Without turning round, I gave a quick derisory wave behind me. I'd found that acknowledging Faith in some small way got her off my back quicker. Ignoring her altogether was like a red rag to a bull (so was trying to answer her back); she just wouldn't let up and that made for a pretty hideous journey. This way, at least, she'd have another couple of swipes, get bored, and start shrieking away with her pals about something – or someone – else.

I think Mum would have had a fit if she'd known what was going on. But then she partly caused it. Up until a few months before, me and Faith would never have dreamt of heading off for school at the same time, but since Dad went abroad to work and Rob left for college last September, Mum insisted that we go together, like we needed the family bonding or something. So off we'd trot, and as soon as the front door was closed, I'd head up the hill to the bus termi-nus and Faith would turn away without a backward glance and make for the lane that led down to the bus-stop by the shops where her mates hung out for her.

6

Generally, there weren't too many people at the terminus that early, so chances were I'd get my spot at the top. Sometimes, if I was lucky, there'd be no sign of Faith when the bus turned the corner into Mile End Road; she was probably in the newspaper shop, I guessed, flicking through the best bits in magazines but hardly ever buying any. Most of the time she *was* there, though, along with the other sixth-formers in their jeans, standing out from all the blue blazers jostling for position as the bus pulled up.

Faith was definitely getting worse – I realized that the previous weekend when I first tried writing to Beth. Just reading the start of that letter back it kind of depressed me. I mean, it wasn't like me and Faith had ever been big buddies (not by about a million miles), but it had gone from annoying but manageable digs (calling me "Conk" all the time 'cause my nose is a bit big, and blaming me for taking the last yoghurt in the fridge when it was her – that kind of stuff) to full-on bitching. Like the endless ripping into me she did in front of her mates. And at home, she only had to see me and she'd let fly with some bitchy comment. I was either lazy ("Hanging round watching those stupid videos again, Conk? Get a life!"), thick ("What are you doing now? Studying for another C+? Dad will be *so* proud!"), ridiculous ("What the hell do you think you look like wearing *that*!") or even, sometimes, a thief ("You've been rummaging round my room again, haven't you?"). It was as if just looking at me annoyed her somehow.

After I read it, I decided not to send Beth the letter; I knew she'd be having a crappy enough time starting at a new school halfway through term, without me moaning on to her. I went out and bought her a stupid Fred cartoon card instead – the kind of thing Rob sent me all the time to make me laugh. It wasn't much, but I knew she'd love it.

"Hurry, Conk! Hurry and play with all your chums! Oh, I forgot. You haven't got any. Still blubbing about your little friend leaving you?" Faith yelled from the back of the bus, as we arrived at the stop opposite school.

I wasn't concentrating properly as I walked down the stairwell of the bus and nearly stumbled. Couldn't go doing stuff like that now, could I? Faith watched me like a hawk for any goofs she could utilize, like when she saw me and Beth in tears and hugging each other the day she came round to say goodbye. She was still milking that one, obviously.

Manoeuvring past all the amblers, I sped through the gates and over to the side entrance of the English block. School. Sanctuary! I never thought I'd have heard myself say that a few months ago.

* * *

"Right, everyone, a couple of things before you go. First, I'm sure you're all hoping I'd forgotten, but today is the day your book reports are due in, and I'm just all a-quiver to read them. I've set a whole evening aside, and I'm sure I'll enjoy going through them as much as you did writing them. Can you pass your work down to the front now, please?"

Mrs Ellis was pretty skilled when it came to sarcasm, like Faith, but the difference was that she did it with a big smile on her face, so you always knew you were part of the joke, not the butt of it.

I bent over, wrestled open the toggle fastener on my rucksack and pulled out the see-through pink plastic folder with my report in it. But before I even unpopped the popper and took it out, I could see that there was a dirty great coffee ring right in the middle of the top page. I froze – how could it have got there? That's why I always kept stuff like essays in the folder – so they wouldn't get messed up. I tried to think back. I'd finished writing my report the previous night, and then taken it through to Rob's room to use the stapler on his desk before I put it in the folder. This morning, I'd come down to the kitchen and left it on the table, then went off to find my hairbrush. Then – then I remembered grabbing it and shoving it in my bag just before I left the house. But that didn't make sense.

Suddenly, the vision of Faith's inexplicable Cheshire Cat grin this morning shot to the front of my mind. I must have been away just long enough for her to flip open my folder and deliberately slam her mug down on my homework before I came back. What on earth was she playing at?

"OK, second thing – " shouted Mrs Ellis over the top of the shuffling and squeaking of chairs and the mutterings as everyone passed their reports forward – "is that we've got a new teacher joining the department this morning. His name's Mr Kershaw, and he'll be covering for Mrs Connell while she's off on maternity leave. Those of you who take drama class will meet him soon enough, but he's asked me to mention that he's keen to start up an after-school drama group once the Easter break is over, and wants everyone to have a think about joining, not just those already studying the subject."

"Molly said she saw him this morning and he's absolutely gorgeous," I heard Sarah whisper noisily to Jamila behind me. My ears pricked up. A good-looking teacher at our school? About time. We'd more than fulfilled our quota of middle-aged, pot-bellied male teachers – shouldn't we be due a break, according to the law of averages?

The bell rang for interval, and I found myself taking the long way round, past the English department's staff room. I was trying to stroll casually, but had to go up on tiptoe to get a peek through the glass panel of the door. I could make out . . . the back of a head. A dirty-blond, longish curly-haired head. The shoulders and collar of a grey cord jacket. It had to be him – no other member of the English department looked like that. Now, if he'd only turn round. . .

Suddenly the door was yanked open and Miss Abrahams was staring right at me.

"Can I help you, Christine?" she asked with a hint of a smile. Then I realized that in full view of the intrigued tea-drinking staff – including a grinning cute face surrounded by dirty-blond curls – I was frozen on tiptoe, mid-step, with my neck craned for maximum nosey-ing. I must have looked like a flamingo in a school blazer!

"No, it's fine, Miss Abrahams," I said, lowering myself with as much dignity as I could muster and slinking off down the corridor.

My first sighting of Mr Kershaw and his first sighting of me. Oh, the shame!

"Christine! Faith!"

Poor Mum! She'd only recently managed to stop herself from shouting Rob's name along with ours when she came in from work. Mind you, she might as well have given up shouting out for Faith; she was never at home after school – she

<blockquote></blockquote>

was too busy hanging out with her posse of fellow witches.

"Up here, Mum!"

I was in Rob's room as usual (it was so much bigger and comfier than mine, and being there made me feel closer to him somehow), with my homework spread out in front of me. Not that I'd looked at it yet – I was too busy gazing out of the window at the tangle of flowers and bushes in next door's garden while day-dreaming about all the cool moves I could have made in front of Mr Kershaw, instead of coming on like some reject from *Riverdance*, that corny Irish dance show that Gran used to love.

Hearing Mum's footsteps coming up the stairs, I snapped myself out of it, picked up a pen and tried to look industrious. She'd been pretty snappy lately, and I knew it would bug her to see me slouching about and slacking on my homework.

"Here you go – another postcard from Rob," she said, coming into the room and holding out a card with Scooby-Doo on it. Taking it, I flipped it over; apart from the name and address, there was only one big word on the message side – "ARE". I picked up the garishly coloured postcard of Elvis Presley in a Hawaiian setting that had arrived from him on Saturday and looked at the one word on that – "HOW". Yep, Rob was definitely sending me some kind of message –

just a particularly slow one, by the looks of it. I burst out laughing.

"Well at least Rob's better at keeping in touch than your dad is, even if it is just with mono-syllabic postcards," said Mum huffily. It wasn't really true: in the two months that Dad had been away in Indonesia, he'd phoned just about every week, and he'd already explained to Mum that it could sometimes be hard to phone from the oil rig because there were so many other people queuing to use the few phones there were.

Mum headed out of the room, then stopped and turned in the doorway.

"Chris, do me a favour and give the garden a quick water before you start your homework, would you? It's been so dry lately and I don't want your dad to think we've been neglecting his precious garden while he's been gone."

"Sure, Mum," I said, jumping to my feet. Well, getting the chance to eavesdrop on the new neighbours next door (who had very good taste in music, by the sounds of it) or doing my history homework – not much choice, was there?

Flicking the spray of water back and forth over the hydrangeas in time to the strains of some groovy track that I couldn't quite recognize coming from next door, I wondered again who our new neighbours were. Mum said she hadn't seen anyone come or go yet in the two or three weeks they'd been there, but by the sounds of muffled voices through the walls and the music playing, there was obviously a full household. Maybe this family had a cute music-mad son who would be only too keen to meet a prettyish sixteen-year-old with brown hair, freckles and a slightly biggish nose. Who was I kidding? More likely he'd be into her very pretty blondish older sister with the big boobs. . .

"Watch it!" said an irate voice from the other side of the fence.

I looked at the hose and realized I'd been spraying most of next door's garden as well as my own. I pointed the nozzle down and peered over the top of the fence. "Sorry!"

Sitting cross-legged on the tiniest patch of grass amongst the wilderness of shubbery sat a girl with long, straight red hair, wearing a huge holey old jumper and a long plum-coloured crushed velvet skirt. In one hand she held a paperback copy of *Pride and Prejudice*, and tucked under the other arm was a bemused-looking fat ginger cat. The girl, the book and the cat were all dripping wet.

"You've soaked the cat!" she said, looking angrily at me.

"It's my cat!" I answered stupidly. Great! This girl was obviously the new neighbour I'd been dying to meet, and all I could say was that it was my cat, like I was allowed to soak him or something. She'd probably run straight into the house and call the RSPCA.

"Hi! I'm Laurie. So what's fat boy's name?" she asked, smiling, squeezing a bedraggled Gus.

"Gus," I managed to squawk.

And that's how I met my new best friend.

Sorry, Beth!

Chapter 2

I automatically went to put my rucksack down on the floor, but then I noticed the half-dried, half-still-sticky puddle of beer in the corner. At least I *hoped* it was beer. Quickly, I moved over to the other front seat of the bus, before the driver started up and did his famous rally-driving manoeuvres that sent any dawdling passengers flying down the aisles.

Settling down on the scratchy bus seat, I pulled out the postcard that had arrived from Rob that morning from the side pocket of my bag and re-read it. Not that there was much to read. Obviously one in a set of three, this particular card was a cheesy soft-focus photo of a ginger cat, surrounded by flowers (supposed to look like Gus, I presumed, minus the battle-scarred nose and chewed ears), with the word "YOU?"

scribbled in Rob's ropy handwriting. I'd have to pin it up along with the "HOW" (came on Saturday) and "ARE" (came yesterday) cards on my pinboard later. It was true what Mum said about Rob – he had been spectacularly rubbish at letting us know exactly how he was doing at university, but at least the constant stream of silly stuff he was sending me made it look like he was in good spirits.

"What are you reading, doughball – your Ladybird books?"

Well, what do you know! Faith was on the bus. Those digs about me being thick, they really got to me sometimes. It's not that I was out-and-out terrible at any particular subject (I just didn't manage to get above a C mark too often, that's all), but I never resented the fact that she was so brainy she could pass tests and exams with obscenely little effort, so why did she go on at me? Older, prettier, smarter, yet still Faith felt she had to needle me. I didn't get it.

"What's this, then?" Faith took me by surprise and appeared right behind me, snatching Rob's card from my hand. Twisting round in the seat, I tried to grab it, but she leaned backwards away from me, just out of reach. She scanned it quickly, with a scowl, then turned to her cronies at the back of the bus, holding the card aloft.

"Aww! Look at this! Our big soppy bruv has sent the ickle baby of the family a cute ickle card.

17

And he only put one word on it," she stood up, tossing the postcard over her shoulder at me, "because that's as many words as she can cope with at one time."

I saw her sashay up the bus like she was some supermodel on a catwalk, to the sound of her mates cheering and clapping, before I leant over, tears stinging my eyes and scooped the postcard off the grubby floor. If Beth was here, Faith would never have done that, but picking on someone who was on their own was so much easier.

I was going to have to think about starting to walk to school at this rate. Who needed major stress at quarter to nine in the morning?

"OK, and what do you think the author was trying to get across here, Samantha?"

I could see Sam Reid cross and uncross her legs and toss her hair back as she tried to come up with an answer for Mrs Ellis. It was pathetic to watch. Sam did this flirty girlie number all the time – positioning herself on the benches by the sixth-form block in case any of the older boys were strolling by was a particular favourite of hers – but why she thought it would work on Mrs Ellis, God only knows! The irritation was obvious on Mrs Ellis's face.

"A simple 'I don't know' would do, Samantha," she barked. "Now, anyone else?"

I felt myself drifting off. I'd answered two questions (correctly, amazingly enough) earlier on, so I reckoned I was off the hook for a while. I was still burning up about Faith's little party trick with the postcard; I felt like she wasn't only having a go at me now, but taking the mick out of Rob too. He didn't deserve that. He always tried to be nice to her, but she was so distant and dismissive with him. You want an example? Well, at Christmas, Rob – a broke student, remember – gave me the one video I didn't have from the first series of *Friends* (we were both mad on old comedy stuff). But Faith changed her mind so often about what she was into that Rob was more or less stuck on what to buy her, so in the end he gave her a twenty-quid gift voucher for Next – clothes seemed a safe bet. As it was, she opened the card, chucked it on to the mantelpiece, and said, "Gee! Thanks for the big effort," before stomping out of the room.

I was boiling mad at her – after all, she'd only bought him a crappy bargain bookshop football annual – but Rob just shrugged, like he always did. Mum made an excuse for Faith again, saying it was her age (what was so hard about being seventeen?), and told us to let it go. But how many times can you put up with sheer rudeness? Other times, me and Rob would be having a laugh, sitting in his room watching some corny old movie on TV. Without fail, Faith would at some point stick her head round the door and make a sarky comment along the lines of: "Oh, look! The couch potato convention's in town again, is it?" or "I'm off out to have a good time with my friends. See you later, Grandma and Grandpa!" If she'd said it with a smile it would be one thing, but smiles were pretty much an alien concept to Faith.

I was getting a headache thinking about her. Now, Laurie – there was someone more interesting to think about. Last night we'd chatted for a few minutes before she had to go in and dry off. She told me she was nearly eighteen and went to St Mary's, the posh girls' school near town. That had surprised me; I couldn't imagine this bare-foot hippy chick in the regimented grey uniform their "gels" were meant to wear. She told me she didn't like it much at St Mary's, but as she'd be leaving after her A levels this summer, she was just cruising along. She and her folks had just moved from Belhurst, which is a super-snoot area, so I wondered what had brought them to our slightly less glamorous neck of the woods. She seemed really cool.

I'd gone back up to Rob's room after I'd talked to Laurie, but I still didn't start on my homework. I was feeling pretty restless, and started rooting around the pile of videos by the coffee-table, looking for something I fancied watching. Beth and I used to love our video nights; we'd hire a movie, or watch one of the many tapes me and Rob had collected, and sit with giant bowls of popcorn or taco chips. She never said it, but I knew Beth particularly liked it when Rob stayed in and watched stuff with us – I always knew she had a thing for him.

I knew what I was in the mood for: the *Friends* tape Rob had given me; it was the one I'd watched the least. Last time I looked, it was somewhere near the bottom of the pile, but now there was no sign of it. I searched through the whole lot twice, with no luck. I realized gloomily that I was going to have to resort to doing my homework at this rate.

Coming into the main hallway at school the next day, I hesitated for a moment, then quickly turned to the yellowing Fire And Safety Regulations that were stuck to the wall with ancient, peeling tape. I don't know how convincing I looked reading them, but I reckoned it gave me a bit of cover while I spied on Mr Kershaw, who was pinning up a poster just along from me.

"Hi! What's that you're putting up there?" I could ask him casually.

"Hi! What's that you're putting up there?" said the simpering voice of Sam Reid – Sam the Slapper, as everyone at school called her behind her back. It wasn't very nice – it wasn't at *all* nice – but she did sort of ask for it, having gone out

21

with a ridiculously large proportion of the male population at our school, as well as a notable amount from Belhurst Boys' Academy, if local gossip was to be believed. And now here she was, doing the hair-tossing stuff for the benefit of Mr Kershaw.

"I'm on the hunt for people to audition for the drama group I'm setting up after Easter. Are you game?" What a voice! A husky Geordie accent, gravelly enough to make you feel like you've had an all-over rub-down with a loofah. Goose-bumps ahoy!

"Absolutely!" trilled Sam, putting her head to one side, all coy. Coy as a black widow spider! I felt like running over to him, grabbing him by the collar of his scruffy cord jacket and dragging him away to safety. Instead, I dragged myself away; it was too depressing to watch the Queen of Flirting in full flow.

I took a deep breath outside in the fresh air. It was probably just as well I hadn't spoken to Mr Kershaw; what would I have said next? "Remember me? I'm the girl who was caught try-ing to ogle you!" Nice one.

Ambling off towards the bus-stop, I spotted Faith over by the sixth-form block. At first I sped up to try and make sure I got to the bus-stop (and, hopefully, on a bus) before she caught up with me, but then I looked harder; she was with her mate Emma something-or-other, who had a particularly vile brother in my year, and she was handing her a video. I felt a sudden cold shudder. It couldn't be my missing *Friends* tape, could it? Knowing Faith, yes it could. Shaking with anger, I started walking towards them. Emma spotted me and nudged Faith. They both stood watching me, arms crossed, muttering to each other and giggling. My heart sank to the soles of my brogues.

"What's up, Conk?" Faith asked with a grin that was about as friendly as a slap in the face.

"Was that my video you gave Emma?" I could feel how hotly pink my cheeks were glowing.

"Don't be so paranoid – I was just giving her back a film I'd borrowed." I knew this was a lie. When did Faith ever sit and watch a video? She hardly had the to patience to sit through a half-hour soap on telly.

"Faith, I really want that video back." I was shaking now, and I knew the combination of the bright red face and the shakes would cause her no end of amusement.

"And what would I want with your stupid video? Grow up, for Chrissakes! C'mon, Emma, let's go." With that, she linked arms with her still-giggling mate and sauntered off. At least she didn't see the hot tears of frustration that had started to trickle down my cheeks.

"Hello again! Are you all right?"

I looked up from the gate catch I was wrestling with and saw Laurie walking towards me in her grey St Mary's uniform – well, her interpretation of the St Mary's uniform. I don't suppose her headmistress was too pleased with the dark grey satin ankle-length skirt and the oversized man's cardie she was wearing. The blazer looked pretty wrecked too, completely frayed at the collar and cuffs.

"I've been better," I said, and managed a wonky smile.

Laurie beckoned me with her finger.

"Follow me. I have an essay that I don't want to do and I'd much rather hear your moans. *And* there's cheesecake in the fridge. . ."

"Faith sounds like a right cow."

"She's not always been this bad. I mean, she used to be . . . well, a *bit* better. Not *much* better, but not as full-on as she is now."

"What's your mum and dad got to say about it?" Laurie asked, walking over to the huge fat American fridge (it looked like it might be roomier than my weeny bedroom next door) and taking out a carton of orange juice.

"Not much. Faith's pretty good at keeping the bitchy stuff for when we're alone. And if I *have* moaned to Mum about it, she tends to make excuses for Faith, and I end up feeling like I'm just some whinging, jealous little sister. And

Dad – well, he's away working so much that we all tend to be on our best behaviour when he's home. He's always such good fun that everybody seems less tense anyway." I scraped up the last mouthful of lemon cheesecake from the wonky star-patterned plate that Laurie had plonked down in front of me.

"What about this brother of yours?" Laurie asked, as she refilled the thick glass tumblers with pineapple juice and cut another couple of slices of cheesecake.

"He's in Liverpool, in his first year studying English. He's brilliant. He knows what Faith's like, but he's too busy with everything for me to go bothering him with stuff."

I focused past Laurie while I answered her, taking in the whole of the kitchen in a nanosecond. It certainly looked a whole lot different to the way it did when Mr and Mrs Harrison and their brats lived here! Their tasteful cream walls were now a vivid sugar pink, and the pine kitchen units were painted apple green. There were a lot more shelves than I remembered too, and all of them were loaded with bits of star-spangled pottery: jugs, bowls, plates, even candlesticks. Laurie followed my gaze.

"It's all Megan's stuff. Stars are her thing this year. Last year it was cats. If we'd lived here then, your Gus would have turned up on a plate or three."

"Megan? Is that your sister?"

"Oh, no. Megan's my mum."

Calling your mum by her first name – that felt weird. It even felt weird hearing Mum and Dad call each other Teresa and Jim. Stupid, but true.

I tried to look blasé.

"Oh, right. So what do you mean: your . . . er . . . mum actually makes these?"

"Yep. She'll be hard at it now, actually; she turned the conservatory into her studio. Do you want to see it?"

Of course I did! A chance to have a nosy round this interesting-looking house with this interesting-looking girl? I was cheering up in leaps and bounds.

Walking along the corridor, I noticed that the fresh jade green paint on the walls gave out halfway along and turned back into the peachy floral wallpaper that Mrs Harrison had been so proud of.

"We've run out of paint – and money, for the moment," Laurie explained, picking at one of the dainty embossed daisies as she passed.

As Laurie pushed open the French doors into the conservatory, I was hit full-force with a blast of colour: sunshine yellow walls (to go with the sunshine yellow sun that occasionally streamed through the glass panelled roof and far wall, presumably), red lino (the only thing of the

Harrisons that seemed to have survived), pots and pots of geraniums (red and pink), bright posters on the walls (one of them of The Beatles), and loads of half-finished bits of pottery, all in various stages of decoration.

Balanced on a stepladder in the middle of all this multicoloured muddle was a very pretty woman with her long hair pinned up messily and an old black track suit covered in paint.

"Megan, this is Christine, from next door. What are you doing up there?" Laurie looked up at her mother, who was teetering very precariously on the top of the steps, waving a sardine in one hand.

"I was waiting for the cavalry to arrive, and here you are. Hello, Christine. You're just the person I need."

At that second I heard a familiar miaow. Looking up, I saw Gus cowering on the top of an old bookcase that reached almost to the roof, next to a matt black stereo speaker.

"What's happened?" asked Laurie, as her mother stepped down to floor level.

"I was just trying out different spots for the speakers – you know how I haven't been happy with the sound set-up yet – when this lovely fat boy followed me up the ladder and has refused for the last half hour to get down. Now, he's yours, is that right, Christine?"

"Yes," I bleated, feeling this woman's hand on

my back, propelling me on to the steps, while stuffing a limp sardine in my hand.

"Go get him, Chris!" Laurie said encouragingly from below.

"While you're up there, Christine dear, could you just manoeuvre the speaker around for me? I'll tell you when it sounds right. . ."

Before I knew what I was doing, I was perched on the top of the stepladder, on one leg, leaning over to tempt a very disinterested Gus with a floppy fish while being deafened by the opening strains of something with a thundering bassline in my left ear. It was in this position, above the noise, that I heard the front door slam.

"That must be Mikey," said Laurie, holding the bottom of the ladder steady.

"Your dad?" I shouted down, guessing wildly.

"Oh, no. He's our lodger."

Above the din of the music I could make out footsteps stomping along the hall towards the conservatory. I wiggled the fish in desperation. Gus looked at me as though I was mad. I heard the French doors creak open.

"Well, hello there!" said the very cute guy in the doorway.

"Hi, Mr Kershaw!" I said, just as Gus made a bolt for the open conservatory door, using the top of my head as a launch pad.

Chapter 3

My pink alarm clock had rattled me awake ten minutes earlier (it was so loud it seemed to vibrate the whole of my tiny room), but I lay motionless in bed, dreading getting up. OK, so I *normally* dread getting up, but this morning I particularly wanted to pull the duvet over my head and vanish.

I'd woken up feeling averagely grumpy, but then a deep, dark gloom descended over me when I remembered my latest encounter with Mr Kershaw the night before. He'd rushed over to help me up when I'd landed with a bump on Laurie's conservatory floor, rubbing my head where Gus had bounced his not inconsiderable weight. As he pulled me to my feet, I found myself unsettlingly close to that grey cord jacket and couldn't help but breathe in his fresh soapy smell (not, thank goodness, aftershave – Mr Trent the geography teacher had a reputation for smothering classfuls of pupils with the over-powering smell of Something-or-Other Pour Homme), together with the less pleasant odour of Eau de Sardine. Breaking away and not looking him in the eye, I started babbling on about get-ting home to check on Gus, muttered a general thanks to Laurie and her mum (what for? Sticking me up a ladder with a fish like some performing seal?) and bolted towards the front door, grab-bing my rucksack on the way.

Mum had looked vaguely interested (for once) when I told her about our new neighbours.

"What colour did you say they'd gone and painted the kitchen?"

"Pink," I told her again, as I lathered my hands with half a bottle of washing-up liquid at the kitchen sink. "Anyway, so then the French doors opened and Mr Kershaw came in—"

"And the pine units are *green*?"

"Yes, and anyway—"

"Those units cost the Harrisons a fortune! Goodness knows what Marianne would say if she could see them now."

I thought of prissy Mrs Harrison, who was ridiculously proud of the house she'd lovingly colour co-ordinated in varying shades of beige. Whatever she'd be tempted to say would probably come out as an ear-splittingly high-pitched shriek.

"And so this lodger of theirs is a teacher at your school?" Mum continued, taking the washing-up bottle from me and handing me a towel.

"Yes, that's what I've been *saying*," I said, gritting my teeth. Why was it so hard to get Mum to concentrate these days? "And the trouble is, he's really, *really* cute."

The minute I said this, I knew it was a mistake, for two reasons.

Mum's face clouded over. "Christine, I don't think it's appropriate for you to have a crush on a teacher."

Oh, where had her sense of humour gone? If I'd told her something like this a few months ago, her eyes would have twinkled and she'd have teased me in that lovely jokey way she had, and probably told me some story about teachers she'd had at school. But here she was going into overdrive like I'd announced my engagement to the guy instead of just finding him – well, visually appealing. Kind of.

"Does Faith know this teacher?" she asked, looking at me in a concerned way. Great! Faith's opinion was of prime importance here, was it? Why did Mum have to drag Faith into everything? It drove me mad. And how flattering of her to assume I was such a babbling love-struck kid that I needed the guidance of my darling big sister.

"Mum, you're missing the point! All I'm saying is that I felt really stupid goofing up in front of

31

him! And what's Faith got to do with anything?" I was just about to discover why bringing up the subject of Mr Kershaw being cute was a big mistake, Number Two.

"If Mum wants me to keep an eye on you, then that's exactly what I'll do," said Faith, leaning on the doorpost, obviously having taken great pleasure in listening in. "And you can bet I'll take a real interest in this teacher from now on. Don't worry, Mum."

What a *top* evening that had been, I thought, as I pulled the duvet up to my cheeks like a security blanket, and snuggled down deeper in bed, trying in vain to ignore the time on the clock. So this morning, all I had to look forward to was *(a)* trying to avoid Mr Kershaw in *every* corridor between *every* break, *(b)* Laurie thinking I was some immature stuttering moron, *(c)* a sister who would try in every conceivable way to embarrass me on the subject, and *(d)* a mother who thought I was about to elope with a member of the teaching fraternity. Great!

As usual, the bus was rollicking along (yes, I *had* managed to drag myself out of bed finally), making it pretty difficult to read my magazine. Glancing at the pages with the reviews of new singles made me think about Laurie's mum (I still couldn't even *think* of her as "Megan", never mind call her that to her face). Imagine having a mum who was into music – and not just stuff like country and western or compilation hits of the 70s, but trendy chart stuff! Laurie was so lucky. The closest my mum got to musical appreciation was humming along to the theme tunes of her favourite soaps.

"Move it, you stupid old woman, for God's sake!" We'd come to the stop by the shops, and someone was obviously losing it with the bus pass lady. It was easy to get narked by her holding up the queue of schoolkids, all just desperate – *naturally* – to get to school, but there was no need to be that obnoxiously rude to her. Whoever was talking that way deserved a good slap.

It was Faith's voice, of course.

I waited to hear the old dear say something about the youth of today, but all I could hear was the stamp of feet and the jingle of money as everyone rushed on board. I sat forward in my seat and peered down below, to see the old lady standing staring at the bus, her trolley by her side, clutching and unclutching a little faded leather handbag. She looked quite lost. Normally, the batty old lady just made me smile. Now, the only emotion I was aware of was the overwhelming desire to twist my rude, ignorant sister's arm behind her back, frogmarch her down the stairs and force her to apologize. Which I wouldn't do, of course, because I didn't have the bottle.

Instead, I sat and waited for the inevitable barrage of jibes that were going to be this morning's source of entertainment for Faith and her delightful friends. Let's see, what would it be first: "How's your new boyfriend, Conk?" or would it be more along the lines of "My sister's into older men, isn't that right, Conk?" I couldn't stand it, not just because all her cronies would be laughing like hyperactive hyenas, but because there were only about a million other people from school on the bus who would be earwigging bigtime if they heard Mr Kershaw's name being barked out.

The muscles in my neck were rock hard with tension as I waited to hear her worst but, weirdly, it never came. Even when the bus stopped opposite the school gates and I made a lightning dash for the stairs, I still expected to get some vitriolic bit of spite hurled at me. But nothing came. Madly, I struggled to work out what was going on – had Faith decided this particular line of torment would be going too far? Maybe, I thought, foolishly forgetting for an instant the true nature of Faith's warped little mind. I quickly looked back at her; she was surrounded by her mates, faces contorted with bitchy giggles, but Faith wasn't laughing. No, she was pushing back her long blonde hair and staring straight at me with an unfathomable expression on her face. Except it wasn't that unfathomable – I knew in a split second that the only reason for the lack of digs was that she was working on some far bigger torture for me, to be put into motion at some later and unexpected date.

With a shudder, I turned away from her and half ran towards the door to the West block, where – it being Thursday morning – a double lesson of English awaited. Deep joy. Not.

I'd just clasped the big brass door handle ready to push when someone yanked it open from the inside, catapulting me forward in one ungainly bound, and causing me to bump straight into the chest of the not-very-ugly Sean Miller, who was in the year above me.

"Oh, I . . . I . . ." Come on, Christine! Spit out something comprehensible, I told myself sternly.

"You all right?" Sean asked, laughing, as he grabbed my elbow. (Be still my beating heart!)

"I . . . uh, I . . ." What was going on? Why had my brain disconnected from my mouth?

Sean laughed again, then stepped around me and was gone. I stood rooted to the spot, feeling the burning heat of my cheeks, and tried to make a word – *any* word – come out.

"Shit," I said, startling myself.

"It's that good a morning, is it, Christine?" said a rough Geordie voice.

"Yes, Mr Kershaw," I managed to mutter. There, look! Practically a whole sentence! Things were improving no end.

* * *

The next day found me flicking through the selection of cards in the newsagent's in Mile End Road. It wasn't what you'd call inspiring: a whole bunch of Get Well/Good Luck/Congratulations!/Condolences jobs all with much the same dusty flower design. It was my own fault that I'd left myself with this dismal choice – I'd forgotten to go to the gift shop at lunchtime and pick up a really good card to send to Rob because, being the Friday before the Easter break, I was too busy gabbing with some of the girls in my class about what everyone's plans were ("Not much", "Nothing really", "Y'know – mooching around"). I was just toying with a pink-rosed, glitter-speckled *Thinking of you* effort that I reckoned might be so bad he'd think it was funny, when a familiar voice made me jump.

"Howdy! I thought it was you. What are you up to?" Laurie looked at the sad collection of cards in my hands.

"Just trying to find something to send to my brother," I replied.

"Well, you're not going to find anything here. C'mon, let's go back to mine. Megan's got a whole box full of stuff she did when she was going through her card designing phase a couple of years back. Let's see if there's anything there that you like!"

"Oh, but I . . . uh. . ."

Oh, but I acted like a fool in front of you, your mother and your unspeakably gorgeous lodger the other day and I'm far too embarrassed to come to your house because of it. Somehow, I just couldn't bring myself to say it out loud.

"Chris," she said, pulling the cards out of my hand and stuffing them back in the rack, "I promise that I won't let Megan force you into any more pet rescue situations." I kind of liked the way she called me Chris – normally I hated anyone shortening my name until I'd known them for about a million years.

"Mr Kershaw—" I began spluttering.

". . .won't be there. Now, no more protests, Chris. Out!"

Laurie took an old plastic bucket out of a cupboard and deposited into it several brushes that had been left soaking in the sink.

"I've told her over and over again not to wash her brushes out here. You think she'd get the message." Seemed like Laurie's mum got quite a hard time from her daughter.

"She used to drive my dad mad with her untidiness." Laurie clicked the kettle on, and I stared at her profile, trying to look for clues as to what the situation was with her father. Was he dead? It just wasn't the sort of thing you blurted out ("Is your father dead, then? Oh, that's nice."). Unfortunately, she looked her usual laid-back self, which didn't indicate anything useful.

"So, why did you dart off so fast on Wednesday?" she asked me, turning round and catching me gawping.

"I just felt . . . you know, ridiculous."

"It was just a funny situation, Chris, not anything ridiculous. There was nothing to be embarrassed about."

"But Mr Kershaw—"

"I suppose that must have been weird for you. I'm sorry, it didn't even occur to me that Mikey was at your school. But that's no big deal, is it?"

Laurie must have noticed the unavoidable pink flush in my cheeks, and tactfully changed the subject.

"So, how's that delightful sister of yours?" she said. "Up to her usual tricks?"

Great! I couldn't tell Laurie that I had an ominous feeling that Faith was brewing up some trouble involving Mr Kershaw. I struggled for something else to say.

"She's kind of laid off me the last couple of days. I get the odd bit of time off for good behaviour, I guess," I answered, stirring a brown sugar lump into my lopsided, star-decorated mug. Then I remembered the bus pass lady. "She did drive me nuts yesterday, though – she shouted at this old woman on the bus for holding her up."

"What *is* her problem?"

"I dunno. I can't actually remember the last time she had a nice thing to say about anybody or anything."

"Was she with a bunch of mates?"

"Oh, yeah – her and her mates only go out in a pack."

"Well, there you go. Showing off in front of your peers – it's a classic attention-seeking device, isn't it? Faith's obviously a very insecure person."

Faith insecure? Had Laurie seen her yet? Faith was textbook pretty: all blondness, cheek-bones and bumps in the right places. If you did a poll of all the boys in school, there's no doubt she'd be mentioned by most of them as top totty, or whatever horrible expression they were using for girls this week. And as for smartness, she'd definitely got more clever genes than me and Rob put together. We both had to swot like mad to get by (Rob with better results than me so far), whereas everything seemed to come so easily to Faith. And it wasn't just academic stuff: Mrs Pirie, the games mistress, had gone on at her for ages to start competing in athletics at local county level, but she wouldn't have any of it. That was the trouble with Faith – everything came so effortlessly to her, but she seemed bored with it all.

So there you have it! Adjectives to describe

Faith: gorgeous, brainy, talented, bitchy and sly. But insecure? No way!

"So you haven't got any brothers or sisters, then?" I asked Laurie, trying to get on to a more pleasant subject.

"Not at the moment, but one's due any day now."

I looked up at her sharply. What on earth did she mean?

"Daddy darling's just about to start another branch of the family tree with his soon-to-be new wife," she said quite calmly.

I took a big gulp of immensely hot coffee and felt it burn its way down my throat.

"So where is your dad now?"

"In our old house in Belhurst. He bought us this place when he broke up with Megan. And that's practically all we got – except me staying on at St Mary's. Megan just went all independent and we-don't-want-anything-from-the-likes-of-him. I'm still not sure whether that was a smart move or not, but we're getting by so far." Well, that explained a lot of things, including the lodger situation.

"Has it been hard on you?" I asked, in my best compassionate chat show host style.

"Well, it made it pretty difficult at school. All my so-called friends seemed to have faded away at a pretty speedy pace."

"Why? Does no one else have parents that have split up?"

"Oh, plenty of them – it's just Dad didn't do it the right way. The respectable thing is to run off with your secretary or some gorgeous young thing from the tennis club. Dad ran off instead with our cleaner, Yvonne," said Laurie, getting up to flick the kettle on again. "Mind you, Megan's so messy that you can see Yvonne's appeal sometimes."

Laurie picked up a clay-soaked, straggly damp rag from the draining board and opened the kitchen window to hurl it out. "Oh, hi, Mikey! You want a coffee?" she bellowed suddenly into the garden.

I jumped, my heart lurching.

"I thought you said he wouldn't be here!" I said, flushing up nicely.

"Chris, you're going to have to get over this shyness with Mikey: you're my friend, so you're bound to be seeing him often enough when you're through here." My God – she knew I had a crush on him! She called me her friend! Talk about mixed emotions. . .

Then, before I could witter any pathetic "But . . . buts", the man himself walked into the room.

"Coffee would be brilliant. I'm wading through a mountain of textbooks and I need something to keep me awake. Ah, Christine!"

He had the sort of smile that made you feel instantly like the most important person in – well, the kitchen.

"You're just the girl I've been looking for," he said, pulling out a chair from the table and sitting to face me, the full beam of those weirdly pale blue eyes focused straight on little old me. My tongue was superglued to the roof of my mouth, but I managed a kind of pathetic "Unggghh" noise and a wan smile in response.

"Laurie tells me you're interested in auditioning for the drama group."

I shot a look over his shoulder at Laurie, who just shrugged her shoulders and carried on making the coffee.

"Well, I—"

"Great. Auditions are on the Monday we start back after the holidays, in the school hall, around half four, so I'll see you there. Right, better get back to the grind and catch some sun while I can."

As he walked out I realized it was the first time I'd seen him without his grey cord jacket on. Instead he was wearing a faded black T-shirt with a dodgy print of a motorbike on it together with some suspiciously heavy metal-style band name. Uh-oh!

"Before you start," said Laurie, shoving a packet of Hobnobs under my nose, "I thought you'd have fun doing something like that. And yes, these are a pathetic attempt to win you over. Take two."

* * *

Kicking off my shoes, I sat cross-legged on the chair by Rob's desk and opened one of the two cards I'd chosen from the pile Laurie had spread out on the kitchen table. For Rob, I'd chosen one with a wobbly gold star on a red background, and for Beth, a wobbly black cat on a gold background. It seemed like stars and cats were the only two designs Laurie's mum specialized in.

I was just about to start on Beth's card – I couldn't wait to tell her about Mr Kershaw and my potential dramatic exploits – when a movement down in the garden caught my eye. Leaning forward I got a full view of Faith, armed with the watering can (last time I saw her with one of those in her hand she was seven years old on a beach in Dorset), wearing a little orange crop top and monstrously tight denim cut-off shorts. What was she doing? Then it dawned on me – Mr Kershaw was sitting on the patio steps, his mug of coffee and pile of books beside him. Faith must have spotted him from the side window of her attic bedroom and decided to get down and mingle. There was no other reason for her to be in the garden: it had been so long since she'd been out in it, I didn't know if she remembered it existed.

Stretching over, I noiselessly opened the window a little further and lay flat on the table, trying to keep myself as inconspicuous as possible.

"Well, hi!" I heard Faith say over the fence to Mr Kershaw, as if she'd only just spotted him.

"Hello!"

"We must be neighbours! I'm Faith, by the way," she said, leaning on the rickety fence and using a strange purry voice I'd never heard her do before.

"I'm Mikey. I lodge here with Megan and Laurie. Have you met them yet?"

"No, I haven't. Do you like it round here? It's pretty dull, but there's a nice pub up the road."

"Is there?"

"And there's even a couple of good clubs up on the High Street. If you ever fancy going. . ." Faith trailed off, leaving her blatant hint dangling in mid-air. How could she go flinging herself at Mr Kershaw like this, all in the space of a few sentences?

"Are you old enough to be going to these places? Haven't I seen you at school?" Mr Kershaw suddenly asked.

"Well, you know how it is. . ." Faith muttered, a bit thrown at being sussed so quickly.

"Ah, right, of course, I've just realized — you must be Christine's sister," he said in a cuttingly cold voice. Could it be that Laurie had told him about Faith and what she was like? He was standing up now and scooping up his books.

"I better get going. Got a lot of marking to do tonight."

I could just see him disappearing into the conservatory, then gasped as I became aware of Faith glancing up towards the window where I was crouching. I couldn't tell if she saw me or not, but next thing she turned and called Mr Kershaw back.

"Actually, I *knew* your name rang a bell."

I flattened myself further on the table and felt my heart race. She was up to something.

"I *was* wondering why my sister was writing the name 'Mikey' in heart-shapes all over her books this week."

The liar!

"It all makes sense now. Christine's got a terrible crush on you, you know. You'd better watch her."

I heard a deep gurgled groan come from somewhere, then realized it was me. Right this second I couldn't see how I was going to lift myself off the desk, never mind step outside my house ever again!

Chapter 4

"No way! No way *at all*. Nope. Not after that humiliation."

Laurie bounded over and held a dripping paintbrush worryingly close to my face. I suddenly felt like I was a contestant on one of those You're-About-To-Get-Gunged! games on Saturday morning telly – which, funnily enough, was blasting away in the living-room right at that very moment.

"Listen, Chris, Mikey's probably seen enough immature pupils playing silly games to suss out what your sister's up to. Forget her. You *are* going to go to the audition, because Mikey's a brilliant person and you'll have a great time in the drama group."

"But what if I fail the audition?" I bleated.

"You tell him that if you don't get a part in the

46

play itself, you'd like to help out backstage, doing lighting or make-up or whatever's going. Now, are you going to help me finish painting the hall and stop finding problems with everything, or am I going to have to stick this brush up your nose?"

"OK, OK – I'll go for the audition. I just—"

Laurie wafted the paint brush menacingly under my nose.

"I'm just saying—"

The brush was so close the paint fumes almost made me gag.

"All I mean is—"

Laurie flicked the brush with her finger and sprayed a few specks of jade green paint on to my face.

"Right, I'm painting, I'm painting!" I spluttered, turning back to the task of covering up the Harrisons' handiwork. Laughing, Laurie chucked me a damp cloth.

"Clean yourself up – I don't like my workforce to look untidy."

It was a bit too late for me; the paint speckles were nothing compared to the swathes of jade green covering my old T-shirt, leggings and most of my hands. Laurie by contrast looked very artistic – just like her mum. Her hair was tied back in a loose pigtail with pretty tendrils escaping here and there, and her baggy grandad shirt and Indian print shorts were spookily paint-free.

"Thanks for inviting me over, Laurie. It was brilliant to have an excuse to get out of the house. I think if I'd seen Faith today after what she said to Mr Kershaw last night, I might have had to ram that watering can down her neck."

In fact, after Faith's little party piece I hadn't come out of Rob's room till I heard her thundering up the stairs to her own room. And Laurie had come through to ask me to help decorate the hall – promising that Mr Kershaw had left at the crack of dawn for a few days' holiday – long before Faith had got out of her pit this morning. Committing yourself to spending the first part of your Easter holiday working might not have been everyone's idea of a good time, but as far as I was concerned, hanging out with Laurie in *any* way was a much cooler option than hanging out aimlessly at home.

"Well, thanks for helping me with this. It's going to be a brilliant surprise for Megan to come home and find the hall finished."

"Where did you say your mum's gone for this craft fair?"

"Bath. She should be in a good mood when she comes back – she's always sold bucketloads of stuff there in the past. And at least this is the first year she's not had a battle with my dad to go. He always hated doing the craft fair circuit. He was such a snob about the whole thing."

She spoke about her dad so casually, like he

was a naughty little schoolboy rather than the grown man who'd broken up her family. I couldn't imagine what it would be like to have your parents split up. What if it happened to my mum and dad? Mum had been acting pretty weird lately. . . It made my eyes fill up even thinking about it. I sniffed and blinked quickly to make my tears disappear.

"So when's the baby due?" I asked, trying to sound as casual as Laurie about the subject.

"In the next couple of weeks or so. Dad doesn't tend to talk about it when he calls me. I think he thinks I'll get upset or something. Hey!" she suddenly said, turning to face me with her usual enthusiastic grin, but, it has to be said, slightly watery-looking eyes, "Do you want to have a breather? I'll show you some photos of him if you like."

I hadn't seen Laurie's room yet. After the manic and mad colours in the rooms downstairs it came as a bit of a shock – plain white walls, white cotton blind at the window, fat white duvet on the bed. Apart from the dark wood of the assorted collection of second-hand chests of drawers, the only bit of colour came from the many clip-framed photos round the walls: some normal-sized prints overlapped in montages in A4 frames, others individual shots blown up. I walked towards one print and looked closer.

"That's me, my dad and Megan on holiday in New Mexico a few years ago," Laurie explained, as I studied the blow-up. Standing in front of a flower-festooned red adobe building stood Laurie, looking about twelve or thirteen, smiling broadly, her braces on show. There was her mum, wearing what looked like a mixture of right-on Native American turquoise and silver jewellery and a pure British Victoriana white antique cotton dress, her waist-length hair flowing out in the wind. Next to them was this dark-haired man in jeans and a denim shirt. He looked wildly uncomfortable. He looked like he was born to wear suits. Suddenly it became very clear why Laurie called her mum "Megan" and her dad "Dad". I couldn't think what those two would have had in common to make them go out in the first place, never mind stay together long enough to bring up a daughter.

"Well," I said, struggling to say something positive, "it'll be lovely to have a new brother or sister to get to know."

"Yeah," said Laurie, grinning at me wickedly. "Maybe we'll be as close as you and Faith. . ."

If you asked me what Mrs Ellis had been droning on about for the previous hour I wouldn't have been able to tell you. But it wasn't just my usual first-day-back-after-the-holiday blues: the whole of the last lesson my stomach had been churning like crazy, anticipating the four o'clock bell, which meant only one thing: the drama group audition.

All through the holiday, when we'd hung out together almost constantly, Laurie had tried really hard to convince me how much fun the drama group would be, but I still couldn't get a handle on my nerves. Of course, we hadn't spent the whole two weeks wittering on about the drama group – a (reluctant) bit of swotting aside, we'd had a brilliant time going shopping in the West End (bought nothing, laughed at the prices in a couple of posh designer shops), nosing around at a photographers' gallery (I'd have been too scared to go in on my own, but Laurie had been there heaps of times), and sitting in cafés swapping life histories. She'd told me about her gran in Wales who ran a wildlife sanctuary, and who she'd escaped to on the odd weekend when things got too heavy at home during her parents' breakup. I'd told her about my gran who was passionate about wrestling and always knitted jumpers no one liked, and how much I missed her since she'd died last year. She'd told me about the A levels she was sitting, and the photography course she was due to start after summer. I'd told her about the GCSEs I was hoping to scrape through, and how I hadn't a clue what I wanted to do after I left school.

I glanced at my watch again. Ten to four. Help!

While Mrs Ellis wittered on about some John Donne poem (which I quite liked, but nerves meant I wasn't going to pay attention to a bomb dropping, never mind a 17th-century poet), I sneaked a look into the little mirror I kept in the pocket of my rucksack. I did a quick snarl: teeth were fine, no remnants of poppy seeds from lunchtime's roll. Face: a bit white through nerves, but OK-looking. Eyes: no smudgy mascara (phew!). Hair: a bit wonky, as usual, but it would have to do. Nose: biggish, as usual. The only thing I couldn't check was my voice. I had this sinking feeling that the minute I tried to speak I'd sound like an asthmatic mouse. Still, I couldn't back out now, much as I'd have loved to.

I peeked round the door of the hall and saw a couple of people chatting to Mr Kershaw. Only two people. How could I hide away at the back when there were only another two bods there? I was tempted to close the door quietly and slip away down the hall, but I was spotted.

"Come on in, Christine!" said Mr Kershaw, waving me over. "Do you know Sean and Lewis?"

What's a girl to do when she's faced with the smiling faces of the coolest teacher in the world and the two cutest boys in school? Talk rubbish, that's what.

"Yes! Well, no . . . it's just, y'know, I've seen you both around. Sometimes. Here and . . . er . . . there."

Stop talking *now*, Christine!

"Yeah, you're Faith's sister, aren't you?" Sean knew who I was! Miracle of miracles! Then I watched as his eyes slid all the way down me and back up again. Obviously doing a quick mental comparison of the two of us. One of us being nearly eighteen, blonde and gorgeous, and the other only just sixteen, hair brownish, looks average-ish. Kind of tough to choose between us, if you were a wildly handsome, fancied-by-every-sane-person-at-school seventeen-year-old boy.

I was spared further strained conversation when another batch of people arrived, among them – groan – Sam Reid, practising her well-rehearsed hair-tossing routine.

"OK, folks – what we're going to do here is work in pairs," Mr Kershaw began, taking off his jacket and throwing it on a chair, like he meant business. "I don't want you to do anything from scripts today; all I want is for you to tell each other about your best friend. That's all. Don't feel you have to come up with anything especially witty or clever; all I'm looking for is to see how well your voice carries, and how you react to working with other people." He smacked his hands together. "Right! First volunteers, Christine and Sam, I think. What about it, girls? Ready?"

No. But I found myself up on the stage

anyway, facing a girl I didn't really know and didn't really like, and not sure what the hell I was going to say.

"Christine, you begin. Tell Sam about your best friend." I didn't dare look down at Mr Kershaw as he spoke; I couldn't face seeing everyone else down there staring back up at me. Instead, I shoved my hands deep in my blazer pockets where no one could see them shaking, and looked straight at Sam. I cheered up a little bit when I realized how nervous she seemed – her bottom lip was quivering like crazy.

I can't really remember now what I said exactly – the adrenaline was pumping round so fast that it made the whole thing a blur – but I know I managed to surprise myself by assuming I'd be talking about Beth, but instead opened my mouth and talked about Laurie. Which was mad considering I'd only known her three weeks.

If my audition was a blur, then sitting down to watch the others do their thing was a double-decker blur with cheese on top. My heart was racing and I felt so strangely excited that all I was aware of was that Sam had spoken about her boyfriend Gavin being her best friend (a poor choice on her part considering he'd been boasting about how far he'd got with her to any-one who'd listen round school lately), and Sean and Lewis telling each other why they were best mates, which was kind of sweet and kind of nauseating at the same time.

"Thanks, everyone," said Mr Kershaw, bringing me back to reality. "I'll let everyone know what the score is by the end of the week."

The end of the week? Who cared? I was just so relieved that I'd actually managed to get up on stage and say something without fainting, and knowing I never had to do it again. Unless I got picked, of course.

"Dad?" I squeaked down the phone. I could hardly believe it was him: it was ages since we'd talked. The last couple of calls he'd made direct to Mum at work, due to the time difference and the shifts he was working.

"Babes!" he yelled at me. "How's my girl?" He sounded scratchy and faint, like he was talking down a tunnel.

"I'm great, Dad! I've made friends with the girl who moved in next door, and I went for a part in the school drama group yesterday!" I sounded silly and giddy from sheer nervous excitement, which I guess is what happens when you've spent a lot of time with someone whose parents have split up. "When are you due home, Dad?" I asked, hoping he couldn't hear the choke in my voice.

"Should be about six weeks' time, if everything goes to plan. Listen, Chris, the line here's really bad at the moment; it could go down at any time. Can you stick your mum on for me?"

As Mum hurried through from the kitchen where she'd been working on her accounts, I made eye contact with Faith, who was sitting in the living-room, staring over the back of the sofa at me.

"Hey, c'mere," she said beckoning me away from the hall and Mum's chatter. I walked as far as the doorway and leaned against it casually, as if what she had to say to me was of infinite irrelevance. Which, of course, it wasn't.

"So, I hear you went for an audition with Mr Kershaw. That's cosy," said Faith, a malicious grin on her face.

"Yeah, *really* cosy, considering it was me, him and about thirty other people." I hoped I sounded tough and uncaring. Fat chance!

"What's the play, then? A love story? If you get a part, will you be going next door for private rehearsals? Ooh, I'd better let Mum know what's going on."

Naturally, I lost it.

"*Nothing's* going on, right! I don't even want to be in this stupid play! So there!"

So there! The weakest pay-off there ever was! Faith's giggles were ringing in my ears as I turned and ran up the stairs. I wasn't even aware that the phone was ringing again.

"Chris!" said Mum. "It's for you. Your dad got cut off, so make it quick in case he's trying to get through again."

I bounded down the stairs two steps at a time, and grabbed the receiver from her.

"Hi, I heard all that, by the way," said Laurie. I cringed automatically, obviously because Mum wasn't exactly subtle, but more importantly, had Mr Kershaw told her I'd talked about her in the audition? "So I'll make it quick," she continued. "First, have you got some good news to tell me?"

"No," I answered, flummoxed as to what exactly she meant.

"What? No good news on the notice-board at your school?"

"Er . . . not that I've seen. . ." I suddenly got an inkling. Could it be true? Had the results gone up that quickly? I'd been planning to leave it till Thursday to check out the notice-board, just so I didn't look too desperate.

Laurie sighed good-humouredly. "Well, Mikey said he pinned up the names of those who made it to the drama group earlier today, and you're on it." I felt the blood drain from my cheeks and saw Mum look at me strangely. "And second – since I've got to get off the line – it's my birthday on Friday, so keep it free. I've got something special in mind."

My heart was pounding – I'd passed the audition, and I was going on a "special" night out on Friday. In the not too recent past, this kind of news would have had me screeching round the house, excitedly telling Mum (who'd have laughed), Dad (who'd have twirled me round), and Rob (who'd have made a big joke of it all). Now I looked up at Mum, who was sitting back at the kitchen table, watching me with a worried expression, then over at Faith, who was still staring over the back of the sofa at me.

"Fine," I said, flatly. "I'd better go."

Chapter 5

Flicking through Rob's CD collection, I found an old indie compilation that had loads of brilliant tracks on it – perfect for dancing round the room to, trying on loads of different outfits and getting in the mood to go out. What kind of night out? I still had no idea – Laurie hadn't budged an inch all week and wouldn't let on what was happening. But even though it was still a mystery to me, as far as Mum was concerned we were just going out for a meal. She was in such a weird, overprotective mood that it seemed like a safer bet to tell her something specific rather than get her all worked up about who knows what.

I'd dragged through a few different bits of clothes from my room to Rob's. Apart from the fact that I practically lived there anyway, he had a great full-length mirror on the inside of his wardrobe door. Hauling myself into my favourite black Levis and a vest top, I yanked at the chunky orange glass handle and pulled the door open to survey myself. But there was no reflection, only a life-sized poster of Pamela Anderson staring back at me.

"*Caught!*" said the felt-tipped pen words scribbled on the badly cut-out speech bubble taped to Pammy's mouth. "*Your brother Rob told me you'd come a-rummaging in here, madam – now hands off his smelly old trainers. They're mine, right?*"

"You're welcome to them, Pamela, but I'm afraid you've got to go," I answered the poster back, peeling her Blu-tack off at each corner. I hated to get rid of a typical Rob-ism like this (he'd booby-trapped the whole room with a whole load of similar stuff) but I really needed the mirror – I wanted to look my best for my night out. Anyway, I thought, sweet as these surprises were, it would be nice if Rob actually phoned from time to time. Yikes! I was starting to sound like Mum. And who was I to talk, when I hadn't exactly been Penpal of the Year so far to Beth?

Once Pamela was rolled up and stashed on the top of the wardrobe, I turned back to the mirror. I usually felt pretty good in this outfit, but now I worried that I wasn't dressed up enough. Laurie had been no help at all. "Don't worry, just wear something you feel good in," she'd advised. Fair enough, but when you could be doing anything from dancing to tenpin bowling to finding yourself involved in a midnight hot-air balloon trip with jugglers (to be honest, I wouldn't put anything past Laurie) it was pretty difficult to make a good judgement call.

I quick-changed into my floor-skimming blue cotton dress. Nah – I looked more like I was off to a family wedding. And a dress might be pretty impractical if we ended up paint-balling. Then I suddenly remembered a dusky pink fitted satin shirt I'd got in the sale at Top Shop. I'd never had a chance to wear it yet, never had anywhere posh enough to go, but if I wore it with my Levis, I'd solve the problem: smart yet casual, as Gran would have said. She liked her little sayings, even if she didn't quite get them right all the time. "Well, look at you three!" she'd said once when we were little, decked out in triplicate in identical Aran jumpers that she'd knitted for us. "Just like Tweedle-Dee and Tweedle-Dum. . ."

I darted back to my own room across the hall and began prising apart the jangling hangers that were stuffed into my tiny built-in wardrobe. There it was – a slivery flash of satin, jammed right at the end of the rail. Brilliant! I pulled out the shirt and gave it a quick once-over, praying it wouldn't need ironing (*big* bore), when suddenly my eye settled on the obvious smear of make-up round the collar. Panicking, I glanced all over it, for other unexpected signs of wear. And there it was – a burn mark on the sleeve, where someone had obviously brushed a cigarette. I held it close and breathed in – it reeked of smoke!

With the shirt bunched up in my hand, I stormed downstairs. Faith was watching telly – in typical Faith fashion – flicking the remote control every few seconds. Just as well she wasn't epileptic! I was relieved to see that Mum was there too, curled up on the sofa, a bundle of work-notes on her lap.

"Faith! You've worn this shirt!" I blurted out.

"No, I haven't," she answered in a bored tone, not even bothering to turn round to see what I was holding.

"Yes, you have! It's got a cigarette burn mark on it and there's make-up on it too!"

"Look, no offence, but your taste in clothes is rubbish. You'd never catch me wearing one of your poxy shirts."

I glared at the back of her pretty blonde head and felt the urge to rush over and yank her by the hair. Hard.

"The only time I've ever had this on is in the changing room at Top Shop, so how do you explain how it got in this mess?"

"It's not my problem, sister," she said infuriatingly, still glued to the ever-changing images on the TV screen.

"There's got to be a simple explanation, Chris, love," said Mum wearily.

"Like what?" I asked defensively.

"Like it was in a sale, Mum," Faith butted in. "And they often put damaged stock in, don't they? Chris probably just didn't notice the marks when she bought it."

"Well, now, that makes sense, doesn't it?" Mum said in a voice that sounded just a little patronizing to me.

"She *did* take it, Mum, I know she did!" I was bleating like a five-year-old, I knew it, but I couldn't stop. "And it's not just this sodding shirt – it's the tape of *Friends* she's nicked and given to her stupid mate!"

"Oh, not *that* again." Faith finally dragged herself away from the screen and looked at Mum with a what-are-we-going-to-do-with-her? expression. "Look at the piles of videos up in Rob's room – it's bound to be in there somewhere."

"Yes, don't be childish, Christine. Your tape will be around somewhere, and you've got plenty of other nice tops to wear."

Childish! I felt my eyes smart, and tried to leave as calmly as I could without saying anything else that would have me labelled as juvenile, and before anyone noticed my "babyish" tears. As I stomped up the stairs, a Poirot-style thought came to me. How could a shirt bought more than two months ago smell so strongly of the night-before's cigarette smoke? See? Not so childish and irrational now! It was just a pity I hadn't thought of saying that two minutes before.

"That's a nice top you've got on, Christine. Blue suits you."

"Oh, thank you," I said feebly to Laurie's mum, who was sitting in between Laurie and me in the back of the cab.

"If you just make a left here, please," Mr Kershaw, sitting in the front passenger seat, told the driver.

My heart was pattering madly and I felt faintly light-headed. After all, I was going out (to dinner, apparently, so Mum could relax) with this very cool girl, her artist mother and my eminently fanciable drama teacher. I lurched from feeling thrilled to feeling vastly out of my depth through the whole journey to the restaurant. Which was stupid really, because it was nothing compared to how *completely* out of my depth I was going to get during the evening.

A very pretty, very tall girl in a minuscule black Lycra dress and eyelashes to-die-for greeted us at the door of Priscilla's.

"Hi! Table for four?" she growled, in the deepest, sexiest voice. As she strolled languidly in front of us I couldn't take my eyes off her legs –

elegant great long things in ridiculously high patent leather platform shoes. It looked like Mr Kershaw was as mesmerized as I was – he nearly collided with a table as we made our way into the restaurant. But then the lighting did seem kind of murky. Subdued, I supposed they called it. Nice, though.

The Amazon woman bent over our table and lit two floating candles in a small green bowl. I noticed a few flower heads floating in there too, and was immediately impressed – I'd never been to any restaurant as posh as this before. Our family were more Sunday-pub-lunch types, or egg-and-chips-at-that-cute-old-fashioned-caff on the way back from day trips. The flashiest we ever got was going out to Pizza Bella on the High Street (Rob's farewell meal – Dad ordered wine and gave me and Faith a glass each as a real treat, even though *he* knew and *we* knew he knew we'd both had a dabble with alcohol often enough before).

"What *is* this place?" I whispered to Laurie as I sat down.

"It's a bit of a restaurant-cum-cabaret," she said casually. "Like it?"

Like it? Yes, the gold columns and red velvet chairs looked brilliant (kind of like an old Victorian theatre); yes, the little stage framed with cherubs was very pretty; but wasn't the main problem that I was under age? Wouldn't I feel the weight of a knowing hand on my shoulder at any moment and get us all chucked out? It was one thing to have the odd cider at a mate's party, but being somewhere as glam and as infinitely grown-up as this was another thing altogether.

"Laurie, I'm sixteen – and only just! Don't you have to be about thirty-five and loaded before you get into a place like this?"

"Relax, Chris. I came here with Dad and Megan for my sixteenth birthday, that's how I know about it." She waved a waiter over confidently as she continued, "And as far as being loaded, well, just this once we are – my wracked-with-guilt father is paying for tonight. Yes, champagne, please." A not-quite-so dizzingly tall but just as striking waitress reeled off a whole heap of names I'd never heard of, and, "Yes, that'll be fine," said Laurie knowledgeably, at one particular suggestion. How did she know this stuff? But then Laurie did come from Belhurst – maybe you just automatically learn about things like how to pronounce *focaccia* properly (Dad pronounces it "that fancy Italian bread") and what *lollo rosso* is (it's some kind of lettuce, actually – Mum and me checked it out in Tesco's once) very early on in neighbourhoods like that.

"Yes, don't worry about it, Christine, just relax and have a good time."

I smiled warmly at Laurie's mum across the table. Thank you, I thought. Thank you for treating me like an adult and thank you for giving me a compliment earlier – two things my own mother didn't seem able to do at the moment.

"So, what d'you fancy to eat, Christine? I'm starving," said Mr Kershaw, scanning the menu.

Food? How could I eat food at a time like this? I was too nervous. And excited. And happy.

First I was afraid, I was petrified. . .

Sounds like it could be me, I thought as the singer belted out the opening lines of *I Will Survive*. Her costume was amazing – a floor-length off-the-shoulder silver sequinned dress with pink silk roses sewn on to the neckline and down the train of the dress behind her. She had on what must have been a wig – the big beehive hairdo was just too humungous and teeteringly perfect to be true.

"Are you looking forward to getting up on a stage, Christine?" said Mr Kershaw, leaning over towards me to be heard, and nodding his head over in the direction of the singer.

"As long as you don't make me sing!" I answered him back, close enough to be aware of that talc smell of his again. I surprised myself at how unfazed I'd started to feel about talking to him, but I realized that might have something to do with the champagne I'd had. Out of the corner of my eye, I could see Laurie topping up my glass again. How many was that I'd had?

"Don't worry, I hadn't got musicals in mind," said Mr Kershaw. "All I want to do at first is work on some improvisation."

Uh-oh! Learning lines was one thing, but the thought of waffling witty stuff off the top of your head made the hairs on the back of my neck stand up.

"I just want us to muck around, see if we can work an idea up into a short play. It's just that there's a community festival happening in a few weeks, and if we can get something together by then I'd like this group to appear."

Before I got the chance to tell him how panicky that made me feel, Laurie's mum waved at us frantically and pointed at the stage. The singing had stopped, and an announcement seemed to be happening.

"Apparently we have two birthday girls in the audience tonight," said the singer in a remark-ably deep voice. Could she be related to the waitress who'd shown us in? "First, can Maria O'Connell make herself known?"

An embarrassed-looking middle-aged woman was shoved to a standing position by her friends, who were whooping like crazy.

"And Laurie Myers – who's eighteen today, folks – where are you?"

Laurie stood up and waved wildly. I felt so

excited I found myself whooping (I didn't know I could) as loudly as anyone in the other party.

"Can we all sing them a quick Happy Birthday?" said the singer, who looked like she was sweating for Britain under the brightness of the stage lights.

As the whole crowd came to the end of the song, conducted by the enthusiastic (and enthusiastically perspiring) singer, Laurie leant over and gave me a squeeze.

"Brilliant, isn't he?" she yelled in my ear.

"Who?" I answered, slightly confused. Did she mean Mr Kershaw?

"Him! The singer!"

"What do you mean, 'him'?" I asked in a tizz, looking from Laurie to the glammed-up person on the stage and back again.

Laurie stared at me and then started laughing.

"Oh, Chris! Didn't you realize? He's a drag queen! Everyone who works here is – the waitresses, everyone! They're all men!"

At that point I felt struck dumb by my own naïvety and knew for certain that I'd drunk far too much champagne. About a bucketload too much, I reckoned.

"That's it, breathe . . . nice and deep, just keep doing that. . ."

Mr Kershaw had been right. As soon as I got outside, the cool night air started to make the nausea disappear. I took several lung-bursting deep gulps of air and let them out slowly.

"Now, how does that feel?" he asked, holding on to my elbow and looking at me in a concerned way.

"Much better. I . . . I. . ."

The tidal wave of nausea caught me completely by surprise, and I only just managed to lurch over to the gutter before most of my fantastic dinner and expensive champagne parted company from me.

Clutching on to some poor person's car to steady myself (I didn't dare look to see if I'd decorated their wheels for them), I felt Mr Kershaw's arm round my waist.

"Oh Christine, I'm so sorry – I guess none of us realized how much you'd drunk." Tell me about it! "Come on, let's go and lean by the wall till you feel better, then we'll fetch the others and catch a cab."

I felt myself shivering madly as the aftermath of being sick and the chill of the air hit me in a oner. Mr Kershaw wrapped one arm around me and fished in his pocket for a paper tissue with his free hand.

"Thanks, Mr Kershaw," I said, blowing my nose and feeling too rotten to take much notice of my sudden physical closeness to him, or the passers-by I was half aware of staring at me. I must have been a vision of gorgeousness –

huddled up and snivelling, with mascara probably smeared halfway down my face and giving off an odour of eau de puke.

"I think under the circumstances you should call me Mikey out of school hours – what do you think?" I looked up into Mr Kershaw's grinning face and managed a wobbly smile back.

"OK, Mikey." At that point I realized someone had stopped on the pavement right in front of us. If I didn't feel bad enough already, a new level of misery was about to be attained.

As if in slow motion, I turned my head and looked into Faith's pinched, white face.

Chapter 6

So this is what a hangover feels like! Like really bad travel sickness combined with that sensation of lying on your back on a playground round-about and watching the clouds spin above you, with a shovel-load of sludge in your head and a funny, furry metal taste in your mouth.

Must remember not to do this again for several years, I thought, as the round paper lampshade on the ceiling twirled back and forth alarmingly. I shut my eyes tight and opened them, trying my hardest to focus. It managed to stay still for a second, but sadly, the same couldn't be said for my guts.

Crawling out of my bed, I wobbled unsteadily towards the bathroom (oddly, my head felt better when I tilted to the left). Clumsily, I tugged off my T-shirt and knickers and stood under the blast of the shower. Bliss!

So, another successful shot at embarrassing myself in front of Mr Kershaw – sorry, *Mikey*. That guy was a jinx. What would happen at drama group? Would I fall off the stage? Have a lighting rig topple on to my head? It seemed just a touch more than likely.

As for Laurie's mum – yeah, she must think of me as an adult now, getting drunk and practically barfing on her lodger! And Laurie must be thanking her lucky stars that she invited me to her birthday do. Not!

I thought back to getting home the previous night. When I'd tiptoed in (*battered* my way in, more like, seeing the state I was in), I'd been relieved to see that Mum was crashed out on the sofa in front of the telly. She'd taken to doing that since Dad had been away, and this time it was perfect for me – chatting nicely about my lovely night out wasn't really high on my agenda. And what of the harbinger of doom? No sign at all of Faith. The speed with which she'd turned and shot off with her mates outside Priscilla's made me feel sure she was doing a marathon sprint straight home to spill the beans to Mum. But so far my luck had held out.

Until I made it down into the kitchen this morning, of course.

"Well, and what have you got to say for yourself?" Mum stood leaning against the sink with her arms crossed and looking brittle enough to break. Faith sat perched on one of the units, her bare feet dangling above the black and white lino. Boy, that was tough on the eyes this morning! Immediately I lifted my head up to get away from the two-tone glare.

"And don't go looking at me with that haughty expression, Christine."

"Mum, nothing's like . . . well, whatever she told you." I wafted my arm in Faith's direction but the sudden rush of movement seemed to send my still slightly drunken blood careering round my body at an alarming rate.

"Christine, I'm *so* disappointed with you! I let you go out for what I assume is going to be a straightforward meal, and then find out that instead you're drunk, at a nightclub and having some kind of fling with your teacher!"

"Mum! That's just not true!" I felt a sudden flush of soberness hit me hard.

"Oh, yes?" She was looking at me like she wanted to slap me. This was scary. "So what are you saying? That you *weren't* drunk?"

Her logic was faultless. "Yes, I *was* drinking. . ." I conceded, "but I—"

"And you're saying you *hadn't* just stumbled out of this nightclub?"

"It's not a nightclub. It's a restaurant with a cabaret. With sort of drag queens and stuff. . ." I trailed off, realizing by how wide her eyes were that I'd said exactly the wrong thing.

"What! You're at some kinky club with your *teacher*. What the hell's going on? And where was Laurie all this time?"

"Inside the restaurant with Megan, her mother," I mumbled.

"My God. It just gets worse! What was this woman thinking about?"

"Mum, it was a lovely night, and Laurie's mum and Mikey didn't realize how much I'd had to drink—"

"*Mikey*, is it? Well, for a start, you can bet you're not going to any drama class with this man, and second, we'll see what your head-mistress has to say about this business next week when I pay her a visit!"

"Mum, you wouldn't!"

"Damn right I would!"

I slammed the door shut and stormed down the path. I had to see Laurie *now* – any embarrassment I'd been feeling had completely evaporated in the light of this new emergency. Letting everyone know that Mum was on the warpath was of primary importance.

I pressed the doorbell and waited. After a minute, I leaned up close against the stained-glass panels, but no, there didn't seem to be any sign of life. Funny, you'd think someone would be in.

Well, one thing was for sure: there was no

way I was going anywhere near home right then. Mum wasn't up for any discussion or negotiation, that much was obvious, and it looked like the best idea was to stay out of her sight and let her calm down.

When did she start getting this angry? I couldn't remember a time when she'd blown up like that at any of us, and all three of us had been in enough stupid scrapes in our time. Like the time when Rob got caught smoking at school and sent home – I think he was only about eleven – I don't remember him getting bawled at; Mum and Dad just sat him in the kitchen and had a big long discussion with him. That's how they always did it with us – you felt so incredibly guilty sitting there across the table from them that you immediately vowed never to screw up again. This yelling thing was weird.

I found myself walking towards Priory Park, where Beth and I used to hang out. It wasn't a very big park, and there was nothing much going on there, but it was kind of nice. Sometimes we'd watch lads playing football or skateboarding round by the old tennis courts (always fun), or we'd just sit in the café and yak – either that or sit on the swings in the evenings when the little kids had gone home. We'd been going there since we met when we started at secondary together, and even when we got older and had more exciting places to go, we'd often end up back at the park anyway.

As I walked through the gates, I saw that there was a fair going up over by the tennis courts. Old trucks and caravans were parked up at the back and a whole colourful assortment of half-constructed waltzers, big dippers and whatever faced the gates.

I suddenly felt swamped by sadness. The fair came to the park two or three times a year, and I'd always gone – sometimes every night it was on. When I was little, Mum and Dad would take us as a treat, when I got older, I'd go with Rob (he always managed to win some dumb soft toy for me), and then it was me and Beth, loving the blasts of music and lights and ever hopeful of bashing into interesting-looking boys on the dodgems. But now who would I go with? Our house had changed from being this great home full of brilliant people – Faith excepted, but when everyone else was there her bad vibes seemed to be diluted – to a half-empty and pretty tense place to be. I never knew what mood Mum was going to be in when I walked in the room, and I never knew in which part of the house I'd stumble across the poison arrows of Faith. And Beth, of course, was long gone.

I slumped down on the grass and lay on my back. I wondered how Beth was doing – did she have moments like this when something happened that reminded her of old times? Or was she too busy getting to know new people and new places to care about me any more? It wasn't as if I'd heard from her, apart from a stupid cartoon We've Moved! change of address card (without a phone number, I noticed. How useless was that?). I knew I wasn't being fair – I told her not to worry about getting in touch for a while if she was a bit frantic with the move and the new school and everything, and I hadn't kept up my end of the bargain by sending her the promised once-a-week letter, but I was suddenly feeling ridiculously sorry for myself. All the good stuff that had happened recently – meeting Laurie, getting to know the best-looking (*only* good-looking) teacher at school, getting picked for the drama group – all this suddenly didn't matter any more. It had been spoiled. All I wanted was to sit watching videos with Rob, hear Mum and Dad laughing in the kitchen, and scream in the pathetic Ghost Train with Beth.

A drop of rain splashed on my nose. Just when I thought it couldn't get any worse. . .

I got up and made a sprint for the shelter by the duck pond as the rain started pelting down. Over at the fair, men were quickly hauling tarpaulins over everything. In the space of a few minutes, the brightly painted machines looked drab and grey, just how I felt. And why, I thought, had this particular sense of gloom descended on me? Well, it all came down to Faith again, didn't it? Good old Faith, telling tales – did I perhaps have my tongue down Mikey's throat in her version of events? Or perhaps he was suggesting running off to Las Vegas to get married by a singing Elvis? And getting a big kick out of landing me right in it. Why? What for?

As kids, I guess she was averagely horrible. She'd pinch my leg constantly when we sat in the back of the car together, and whip away my panda when Mum wasn't looking, holding him out of the window of the bus and threatening to drop him – that kind of thing. I've spoken to plenty of people who said they had older brothers and sisters who were juvenile monsters, but who then turned half-decent when they got older. Faith, on the other hand, showed signs of getting much, *much* worse.

The only time she never acted up was when we used to go round to Gran's – she'd be fussing about helping Gran set the table, like a regular little Girl Scout. When she'd hold out a plate of biscuits and say "Want one?", I'd turn to see who she was talking to, not realizing that it was me. Sometimes she used to spend the weekend at Gran's, and for a couple of days after, she'd be this weirdly pleasant person ("I think Gran hypnotizes her," Rob used to say) before she'd gradually return to her miserable old ways, and I'd have to guard Panda with my life.

I was shivering with cold by this point – I'd

only pulled on my thin cotton skirt and a T-shirt in my rush to leave the house – and decided I might as well head back now, even though it was still pouring. It kind of suited my mood.

As I walked up Laurie's pathway, I could hear my trainers squelching every time I took a step. The back of my skirt was soaking and flapped uncomfortably against my calves, and my wet hair was plastered to my head. I rang the bell – still no one home. With a heavy heart, I turned and squelched my way next door to our house.

Biting the end of my pen, I leant forward across the desk and peered down into Laurie's garden – but the only movement was Gus prowling around, pouncing on microscopic bugs. There'd been no lights on last night either. I felt a bit worried, because Laurie hadn't mentioned anything about them going away for the weekend.

Back in our house, so far everything had been pretty quiet, but that was just because we were all playing a game of avoiding each other. I'd come in after my walk/soak in the park, changed out of my wet stuff and spent the evening (and the night) in Rob's room, and this morning I'd just nipped down to the kitchen (which was empty), grabbed a bowl of corn-flakes, and run straight back up.

I'd decided to spend the afternoon writing letters to Rob and Beth, since I'd had them both so much on my mind, but instead I just sat staring out of the window, going over the events of the last forty-eight hours again and again in my head. Eventually I gave up trying to write, and went over to the pile of videos on the floor, flicking through them and trying to find something to take my mind off my troubles. The main thing that I was trying to avoid thinking about was the business about Mum reporting Mikey to the school. Could he lose his job? Would everyone in school find out about us, even though there was nothing to find out about? I felt sick at the thought of it.

I also felt – well, hungry. Apart from this morning's cornflakes, the last time I'd eaten was Friday night at Priscilla's, and that particular meal hadn't given me much sustenance in the end. I was going to have to risk another SAS raid to the kitchen.

Bad move.

"I was wondering when you'd get around to showing your face."

"Mum, I've just come down for something to eat," I mumbled, not daring to look her in the eye. She was sitting at the table, along with Faith, who had obviously been flicking through a magazine, but stopped with her hand in mid-air now the fun was about to start.

"I think we can forget about food for a moment, don't you? Aren't there more important things we need to deal with first?"

I leant back against the door-frame, to steady myself from shaking, if nothing else.

"Mum, I got drunk – it was an accident! I'll never do it again. But that's all there is to it!"

"Oh, yes? And how exactly do you explain what Faith saw?"

"What Faith saw was Mikey – Mr Kershaw – helping me outside when I felt sick. End of story."

"That's not what Faith says; she says you were kissing and cuddling when she saw you. She—"

"Mum, Faith's a bitch!" I exploded, looking from one face to another – one ashen white, the other stupidly smug. "No, that's not quite right – she's a superbitch! A real champion of bitchiness! Lying, backstabbing – you name it, she's a real expert at it all! In fact—"

"That's enough, Christine! All Faith and I care about is your welfare! A grown man seems to be in danger of taking advantage of you, and she's doing what she thinks is right to stop that from happening."

I leapt across the room and slammed my hands on the table. Mum jumped and even Faith looked shocked.

"*Why* do you have to take her word instead of mine? Why—"

A sudden knocking at the opened back door stopped me in mid-flow. Looking back, I realize how brave Laurie was to come barging in right in the middle of this tornado of a row.

"Sorry to interrupt, but I heard the shouting from our garden and just leapt across the fence," Laurie panted, standing in the doorway. Mum looked quite shaken.

"Laurie, in the circumstances I don't think it's appropriate for you to be here or, in fact, to be friends with my daughter, full-stop." Her hands were trembling round the mug she was holding.

"Oh, I think in the light of what I heard just now, it's *very* important that I'm here." She strode over and pulled out a chair, sitting herself down and facing Mum. Suddenly Laurie seemed very grown-up, much older than eighteen, and Mum, pale and shaky, seemed an awful lot younger.

"Here's the thing, Mrs Woods: myself, my mother and Mikey are all very sorry that Chris got in the state she did. It was just that in the excitement of the night, I kept filling up her glass without real-izing it, and because the show was on everyone was a bit distracted. It was an honest-to-goodness mistake, OK?"

Mum nodded mutely.

"Now, both myself and Megan were planning on coming through here to see how Chris was doing and to apologize to you yesterday morn-ing, but a slight situation arose – basically, my father's girlfriend had a baby on Friday night, and I've been with my dad the whole weekend."

"What did she have?" I interrupted, caught up in the excitement of the news.

"A boy. Anyway, as you can maybe understand, Mrs Woods, this was a bit upsetting for my mother, and she decided she'd rather go away for the weekend, just to clear her head." Again Mum nodded, this time almost sympathetically.

"And finally, this business with Mikey and Chris. . . Well, when we saw that Chris felt ill, I was about to take her out for some fresh air, when a birthday cake arrived, a surprise my mother had arranged. Mikey told us to stay put and that he'd take Chris outside, where she was horribly sick, partly over his shoes." I winced – I didn't realize my aim had been that random. "I don't think she was in the sort of state where he'd have been overcome with any desire to kiss her. And he did suggest to me that the reason Faith might have misinterpreted what she saw was that she was carrying a bag from the local off-licence; perhaps she was a little worse for wear herself?"

Mum looked over at Faith, Faith raised her eyebrows and shrugged her shoulders in a not-guilty protest of innocence.

"And, lovely as your daughter is, Mrs Woods, there's absolutely no way Mikey would ever be interested in Chris: apart from the fact that she's a pupil at his school and he's a very professional teacher who would never abuse his situation, he's already got a girlfriend he's very much in love with – my mother."

84

Chapter 7

The low morning sun caught me right in the eyes, making me squint, as the bus rounded the corner into Mile End Road. I didn't mind though – it was a relief after the miserable rain at the weekend. In fact, I felt giddy with relief this morning (pretty unusual for a Monday).

For a start, there weren't going to be any feverish exposés at school along the lines of Gymslip Girlfriend Loses Teacher His Job. Mum had taken on board everything Laurie had said and backed right down. Second, the tension had eased off at home. Faith made an excuse to leave and go round to her mate's while Laurie was telling us more about the new baby and the budding romance next door, so once Mum and I were on our own, we spent an almost-like-old-times evening gossiping about the goings-on.

Mind you, it took her till bedtime to say the magic words "I'm sorry". She muttered something about just being worried about me, and stuff about Dad and Rob being gone. It didn't make much sense, and it was a bit lame after having written me off as Wild Child Extraordinaire over the weekend. But I was too glad it was all sorted to go getting all pernickety about her apology. I muttered that I was sorry about the drunk thing, and we gave each other a quick, slightly embarrassed hug.

And as a special added bonus this morning, here we were, moving off from the bus stop outside the shops, and Faith hadn't got on. Joy!

"Good effort, Christine."

My heart leapt when I saw the red 70% Mrs Ellis had scribbled at the bottom of my test paper. Not bad! Around 60% was my usual best achievement.

"Of course, if I was a *really* tough teacher, I might have deducted a point for the fact that you managed to misspell your own name in two completely different ways."

I could hear some irritating sniggering coming from Jamila and Sarah sitting behind me,

I looked at the top of the first sheet: "Christine Wods". Second sheet: "Christien Woods". I could see what Mrs Ellis meant – spelling was never my strong point, but getting my own name wrong was bad news. Concentrate – I just had to concentrate harder. On Friday when we'd done that particular test I'd been thinking too much about my mystery night out with Laurie to keep an eye on my errant spelling. No more. No way. Nothing was going to spoil my concentration from now on. I mean, my first drama group was coming up next, and was I thinking about it? Was it distracting me? Nope. But I did start to wonder what would be expected of us. Would we have to get up one by one in front of the others and recite stuff? Would we be expected to learn lines right off? Would we—

"Christine! I realize you're all a-glow at the magnificence of your score, but do you think you could pay just a little attention to the rest of this lesson, please?"

The drama class was just two doors along from Mrs Ellis's class, so I thought I might be first to arrive, but there were already about ten people there, hovering around. I scanned the faces but didn't know anyone very well. A wave of awkwardness washed over me.

"Hi, Christine!" a voice whispered in my ear. It was Sam the Slapper, coming on like she was my best friend, putting her hand on my shoulder. "I'm so glad you're here – I don't know any of this lot!"

But they probably know all about you, with

your reputation! I thought. Mind you, I did feel kind of relieved to have her there to talk to. Just as long as no one assumed that we were actually mates or that I was anything remotely like her.

There was a last minute shuffle of people coming in, which included Mikey. Last time I saw him I had my head between my knees in the back of a taxi. Not that I was able to see much of him from that angle! I felt prickles of embarrassment as I remembered barfing in front of him (and on him). Oh, what a klutz! And of course, there was the fact that he was Laurie's mum's lover. . . That hadn't quite sunk in yet.

"Right, everyone," said Mikey, holding up his hands to get people's attention. "As you know, what I want to work towards is the community festival, which is in six weeks' time. This works out quite well, because it's just before half-term, and after that, it's full-on exam time, as I'm sure you're all too well aware of. Now, I don't want to end up getting grief from other teachers about you neglecting your swotting because of this group, so bear that in mind. Let's get going! Sit yourselves down in a circle and we'll all introduce ourselves. I want each person to say their name plus one thing that really bugs them and why."

First I sat down with my legs crossed, then stuck them out straight in front of me, then changed again, this time swivelling them round to one side. I was finding it hard to take in what the others were saying – Sean Miller was sitting right opposite me with Lewis, and I was panicking that they could see my knickers. I fidgeted and tugged at my shortish skirt, willing it to be longer. Suddenly Sam, who was sitting next to me, started talking. So what was her big hate? Getting her precious hair wet? Breaking a nail? Still, it meant it was my turn next. Uh-oh!

"Hi! My name is Samantha Reid, and I really, really hate people who bitch about you behind your back. They think no one knows, but it's always really obvious."

There was a pregnant silence for a moment. Sam's love life was legendary at school, and there wouldn't have been one person in that room – with the exception of Mikey – who hadn't had a good gossip about what she'd been up to at any given time and who with. Feeling somehow slightly guilty, I decided to speak up fast to break the weird atmosphere.

"I'm Christine Woods, and I can't stand my sister." Should I have said that? There were a couple of people in her year here – were they her mates? Somehow I doubted it. They looked like decent human beings. Well, what the hell! It was out there now. "Some of you might know her. Her name's Faith, she's in sixth form and she's very pretty with long blonde hair. She's got a lot more going for her than I have – and it's not like I've ever been jealous of her – but she seems to get some kind of kick out of hassling me all the time. It's a real pain. Er . . . that's it."

I shrugged, and hoped the next person would start talking, so that everyone would stop staring at me. Not liking being stared at – great qualification for acting, wasn't it?

After my little speech was over, I started to relax and enjoy myself more. Cleverly manoeuvring my rucksack in front of me helped solve the pants-revealing dilemma, and it was fun watching the other girls looking all mushy-eyed at Mikey. If only they realized he liked older women! *Much* older women.

As it turned out, out of the twenty people in the room, the only ones who weren't already taking drama class were me, Sam, Sean and Lewis. Wow! I had something in common with Sean Miller! It wasn't much, but it was a start. Maybe if I ever had the courage to talk to him I'd find we had loads more in common. Maybe.

Before we gathered up our stuff to leave, Mikey told us that we all had to come up with an idea for a short piece, and we'd start talking about them and working them up the next week. He also said we might need to do some extra rehearsals – like Sunday afternoons – since the festival was so near.

"Sounds like fun, doesn't it?" said Sam, linking her arm into mine as we left the classroom. I wished she wouldn't do that. "But I don't know about rehearsing on Sundays – Gavin plays football then, and I know he likes me to be there to cheer him on."

Don't kid yourself! I thought darkly. Gavin is interested in you all right, but it's not your support he's after.

"See you next week!" said Lewis, startling me, as he passed us with Sean. Was that for Sam's benefit? A bit of flirting for the Queen of Flirt? But no, Lewis's grin seemed friendly and real, and it was directed at me. Sean was smiling too.

Not a bad day's work, girl!

"I can't think of a single thing! Absolutely nothing! My mind's a blank!"

"Ooh, I haven't heard this in ages," said Laurie, snapping open a CD case and shoving the CD in the player. "Great room, by the way."

"I know, I love it. I used to come through here all the time to watch TV with Rob, or listen to music. He doesn't mind me using it while he's away – he knows my room's not exactly a palace."

"What's Faith's room like?" Laurie asked, leaning back on the rug.

"I don't look too closely, to be honest. I only ever go in it to get the hairdryer or whatever, and I make it as quick as I can. If she caught me in there I'd be dead meat – I'd get accused of nicking her precious stuff probably. Anyway, I don't want to talk about her – I need your help to come up with an idea for Monday. I haven't got a clue."

"Christine, there are *millions* of things you could suggest. Mikey's not looking for a word-perfect script, you know – only a rough idea."

"But none of my ideas are that interesting," I moaned, curling up defensively on the old sofa. "I don't even know why he picked me for the drama group – everyone must be much better at acting than me."

"Chris, you've got to start believing in yourself a little bit more," said Laurie, pushing herself up on to her elbows. "That's why I knew you should have a go at the drama club. Your darling sister's been chipping away at you for so long that you've lost some of your self-confidence, that's all."

I was slightly stunned. Nobody had ever put it into words – the fact that Faith's bitching wasn't just annoying, it was actually having an effect on me, on my personality. I felt choked and didn't know what to say. I guess Laurie saw how I felt and changed the subject.

"OK, OK. Let's think. What about boys? Something to do with what a pain they are to go out with – they don't ring when they're supposed to, that kind of thing."

"I don't know; I haven't had a boyfriend. The

boys that've asked me out have tended to be jerks. Beth and me used to do this test – if they didn't like the same kind of comedy shows as we did they were out. And none of them ever had the same sense of humour as us. If it didn't have farting in it, they didn't get it. What about you? Been out with anyone nice?"

"Nah, not really. A group of us used to hang out with a crowd of boys from Belhurst Academy, and I ended up going out with a couple of them. But they were both pretty much snobs. They took one look at Megan and thought she was weird – their mums were into coffee mornings and shopping with their Gold American Express cards. Megan would try talking to these guys about music or show them her work and they'd start giggling. So, is there no one cute in the drama group?"

"Well, yes, I guess. There's Sean and Lewis. . ." I couldn't help grinning.

"Oh, yes? More, please!"

"They're in the year above me, and Lewis's kind of cute – freckly and funny. And Sean – Sean's *really* cute. He's got this dark, scruffy hair and this sort of shy, intense look about him."

"Intense? Ooh, I think I prefer the guy with the freckles. I thought you would have too – didn't you just say you liked them funny?"

"Sean's got a nice smile too. Listen, you're getting off the subject. What about something along the lines of what's happened to you? Y'know, your dad having a new family and everything?"

"I think you'd need a six-part drama series to do justice to that one, and you've only got a twenty-minute slot, haven't you?"

"Yeah, I suppose you're right. How's it going there, anyway?"

"Not bad, surprisingly. I think Dad's torn between being thrilled and feeling guilty, but spending last weekend with him made us both feel closer than we have in a long time. And the baby's gorgeous. And it wasn't too awful seeing Yvonne in the hospital, either. Dad was pretty chuffed that we were both making the effort to get along."

"Does he know anything about your mum and Mikey yet?"

"God, no! They didn't really want anyone to know for a while, not till they were sure themselves. I mean, for a start they haven't known each other that long – they were only mates for about six months before he moved in with us, and of course there is the age difference: he's twenty-five and she's thirty-eight. Not that that seems to bother either of them, but they knew it might be a problem for other people, for sure. Anyway, I only told you a little earlier than planned because of all that nonsense Faith came out with. Now let's get back to ideas. Yvonne's coming home with the baby today and I told Dad I'd pop round for a while this afternoon, so I can't stay too much longer."

I glanced round the room for inspiration, and my eye was caught by the card I'd been meaning to send Beth.

"What about something to do with Beth moving away? When your best friend starts a new life somewhere else?" I suggested.

"That's great! Maybe you could just have the old friend narrating at the side of the stage, talking about what their friend is doing, while everyone acts out her new life in the main part of the stage."

"Or *maybe*," I said, suddenly inspired, "it could swap between what the old friend *imagines* her friend is doing – meeting gorgeous boys, going to brilliant places – and how the friend's life actually *is* – feeling awkward, sitting on her own at lunchbreak—"

"That's it, Chris! There's your idea! It could be really funny!"

I loved Laurie's enthusiasm and I loved the fact that I'd come up with a plot. This was good. Maybe drama group would be more than just a chance to drool over Sean Miller.

"Of course you could always put forward an alternative idea, a sort of horror movie," said Laurie with a sly smile on her face. "Like a story about a girl who's such a bitch to her sister that her sister is driven mad and comes after her with a chainsaw one night. . ."

It was at that point we both heard the squeak of the floorboards outside the room followed by the thundering of footsteps running up to the attic bedroom.

Stunned wasn't the word. When Mikey picked my story you could have pulled away the chair I was sitting on and I wouldn't have noticed, I was so surprised. I was even more surprised to realize that everyone in the group really liked it too. In fact, Lewis came up to me at the end of class (trailed as ever by shy boy Sean) specially to say how much he liked it! I was so excited I half ran, half floated into the house. I was dying to tell Mum, but the house was empty.

I was heading over to the fridge to get some juice, still trying to get my breath back, when I spotted the letter addressed to me, propped up against the bread bin. I recognized Rob's hand-writing straight away and tore it open. What a novelty! An entire letter instead of a postcard. What had I done to deserve this honour? I was about to find out.

After lots of funny stuff and the usual waffle, I got to the bit he was obviously working towards:

Chris, I've been thinking about something seriously lately, and you're the only one I can tell – I know you'll understand. I've got to know this guy in his final year on my course, and he's been telling me about how he took two years out to do charity work – he taught English in this remote village in India. It sounds amazing! You go out with a few volunteers and work with people in really impoverished areas, teaching them and working with them. You get bed, board and a bit of pocket money and that's about it, but can you imagine how it must feel making a difference to people's lives? I'd love to do it, Chris, and sooner rather than later. But don't go telling the folks yet – not till I'm 100% sure of what I'm doing. I'll keep you posted.

Love, Rob.

I slouched down on to a chair, completely deflated. How could I stand Rob being so ridiculously far away for two whole years? It was bad enough to have him four hours' train ride away. And when would I ever hear from him? I didn't suppose for a minute that remote, impoverished villages in Outer Mongolia or wherever had any gift shops with a nice line in novelty postcards.

Just what was it with my life just now? Every single time something good happened, something rotten came running up behind it about a second later.

Chapter 8

"He's beautiful," I lied, squinting at the slightly out-of-focus Polaroid of the bawling baby.

"Yeah, yeah, I know he looks like a small bad-tempered tomato in that one, but check out this one — he's much cuter." Laurie passed me up another photo from the pile she had beside her on the floor, where she was putting together another of her clip-frame collages. I rolled over and grabbed the photo, then flopped back down on Laurie's big white marshmallow bed. It *was* a sweet picture — baby Ben seemed tiny bundled up in his proud big sister's arms.

"You'll have to come with me and see him some time. Only bring a spare top with you in case he pukes all over you — that's his party piece. Anyway, speaking of brothers, heard any more from yours?"

"Nope," I answered, drumming my nails against the back of the pic I was still holding.

"Mad at him?"

"Yep."

"How long's that been since you got his letter?"

"Two weeks." I sat up on the bed, feeling suddenly fidgety and ratty. "I mean, it's not fair, is it? You can't announce that you're about to hike off to the other side of the world for years and then go all silent, can you?"

"Can I have that back before you mash it to pieces?" asked Laurie. I glanced down at the photo and realized I'd been bending it back and forth between my fingers. "Thank you. So, have you tried calling him?"

"I can never get through," I sighed. "There's just one communal payphone in his halls of residence, and it's either engaged, never answered, or answered by someone you know doesn't have a clue who Rob is and has no intention of giving him the message that you rang. It's hopeless."

"So you still haven't said anything about it to your mum?"

"Oh no." I slithered off the bed and dropped-down beside Laurie. "She's gone back to being all distant and jumpy – there's no way I'm going to spring that one on her. Rob's going to have to do his own dirty work there."

"Well, I suppose there's always the chance he

might decide against the whole idea."

"I doubt it. It's exactly the sort of thing I think Rob's wanted to do all his life. But I suppose it's my problem, not his. I'm just being selfish – I want him to be around, or at least in the same *country*, so that I feel I could see him whenever I wanted to."

"You're not being selfish, Chris. You've just had a lot of people leave over the last few months – Beth, your dad, Rob. It's only natural that you want everything to stay the same now."

"I guess. . ." The antique clock on her dressing-table gave out a resounding "boing" as it hit one o'clock. "God, Laurie, I didn't realize the time! I've got to get to rehearsals!"

"Yeah, Mikey went out for lunch with Megan earlier, so I guess he's gone straight to the school. Oh, and while I remember," she dragged her bag over and pulled out a battered Filofax, "what day's your performance on?"

"The 22nd," I gulped, as it dawned on me for the first time that people would actually be watching us *do* this stuff.

I padded about on the stage, while Mikey – dressed in his favourite off-duty outfit of the naff heavy metal-style T-shirt – spoke to the only other people who'd arrived so far: two boys who were doing the lighting. I guessed that with it being a Sunday afternoon, people didn't feel the need to do the usual arriving-on-the-dot thing that was expected of them all week. The last time I'd been on the stage was when I did my audition; since then we'd been rehearsing in the drama room. But now it was time for a "proper" run-through – working out entrances, lights, make-up and costumes. I amazed myself by being quite excited rather than excruciatingly nervous.

Of course, it was pretty easy for me – it was safe to say mine was a bit part (thankfully). The two leads were going to be Marianne Stansfield (playing the narrator and friend-who-was-left-behind), and Elise Banks (playing the friend who'd moved away). Marianne was going to stay in one spot to the left, at the front of the stage, to do her part, while Elise flitted between two groups of us in the main stage area. The stage was going to be blacked out, then a rosy pink light was going to shine on those of us acting out the groovy life Marianne's character *thought* her friend was having; then we'd be back in the dark while a blue light came up on the other group doing the "real-life" stuff. Lewis and Sam were in the "blue" group (moaning at, bitching about and generally ignoring Elise's character), while me and Sean were in the "pink" group (laughing, chatting and partying with Elise's character).

Mikey had come up with a pretty funny script, based on all these little sketches we'd improvised. I only had two lines: "You look great! Like a supermodel!" and "Wow! You're amazing!" but I was happy with that. Although there was *one* role I kind of hankered after: during a party scene, Deena Michaels had to hold hands with Sean who, at the end, picked her up and twirled her round, while the rest of us danced and cheered. You should have seen her face when Mikey gave everyone their role! Chuffed wasn't the word. And who could blame her?

A flurry of breathlessness and hair-tossing suddenly announced the arrival of Sam Reid.

"Am I late? Sorry, Mr Kershaw, I was just watching the first half of my boyfriend's football match," she gasped, waving her hand at her face in a pantomime cooling-down motion.

"Relax, Samantha, you're one of the first here. Listen, why don't you and Chris go backstage and start looking through the wardrobe room for costume ideas?"

Sam beamed up at me, and came clattering up the stairs by the side of the stage.

"Come on, Chris! Let's go and bagsy the best stuff for ourselves before the others arrive!" Well, you couldn't fault her enthusiasm, I thought. She could probably make tidying your room up into an excuse for a party.

Opening the big wooden doors to the wardrobe room didn't fill us with the anticipated excitement, though.

"This stuff's so bad it looks like it would be turned down by a charity shop," Sam grimaced, holding out an old-lady-*circa*-1960 balding mohair coat.

"And I don't think much of this lot's seen the inside of a washing-machine for a few years," I replied, flipping through a rail of musty smelling and make-up-stained shirts and jumpers.

"Do you think Mr Kershaw got his T-shirt from here? It's bad enough, isn't it?" Sam grinned at me. I burst out laughing before I could stop myself. Much as I felt a loyalty towards Mikey, and although I was wary of Sam, I *was* starting to realize that Mikey's fashion sense was pretty hit and miss.

"Well, one thing's for sure," Sam went on, "I certainly don't think he's got a girlfriend, 'cause no girl would let him out wearing what he's got on today."

"Actually, he has got a girlfriend," I blurted out. God, why couldn't I keep my trap shut? Sam stopped rifling along the rails and fixed me with a wide-eyed stare.

"Yeah? Tell, tell!"

I had to backtrack fast.

"Oh, it's just that he rents a room from my neighbour, and she says he's going out with someone. I don't know any more than that. Sorry." My inevitable blush was starting up. Lying just wasn't my thing.

"He lives next door? Wow! That must throw up some good spying stories. Get some gossip on him quick!"

If only you knew! I thought, watching Sam turn back to the unpromising rows of jumble rejects.

"Better watch that sister of yours, though. I could just see her giving it all she's got over the garden gate when Mr Kershaw's around."

What was it with Sam? She'd managed to surprise me twice in a matter of minutes. How could she possibly have guessed that that was exactly what Faith had already tried to do?

"What do you mean?" I asked, trying to double-check that I'd picked her up right.

"Oh, come on, Chris! It's right up Faith's street, isn't it? She likes to be queen bee with all those horrible mates of hers, and she loves the fact that every boy at school's hormones explode when she's around, even though she never goes out with any of them. In both cases, what could be cooler than everyone knowing she had Mr Kershaw panting over her?"

"OK, so who are you girls bitching about?"

We both spun around to face Lewis, whose freckled nose was scrunched up as he laughed at us. Right behind him, smiling sweetly, was Sean. I felt my heart lurch into the equivalent of a forward tumble. Sam's reaction was to toss her hair back — it must be a reflex action when boys are around. She hadn't done it once when we were alone together.

"We were bitching about Christine's sister. It's a family thing – she's allowed," said Sam defensively.

"You don't give your sister a very good press, Christine," Lewis laughed, pulling a plastic chair off a stack and making himself comfy. Sean stood leaning against the door. It was him I wanted to have eye contact with, but of course it was mouthy Lewis who was asking the questions.

"Well, she doesn't give me much of a life," I answered him.

"Faith, Faith!" Lewis muttered dreamily, clutching his hands together over his heart. Oh, here we go! I thought. Another bloke for her fan club. "A beautiful name for a beautiful girl. Pity she's such a miserable old witch."

This was a day of revelations! Other people were aware of what my darling sister was like. I wasn't alone. What a great feeling!

"You know something? I think Elise is right, we do need another character in that scene."

We all stopped and waited to see what Mikey would come up with. So far we'd got halfway through our play – it would take up only ten minutes on the day but had taken us the best part of two hours to run through so far, what with the tweaks, changes and lighting try-outs.

"If you could give me a minute just to have a

quick think about this," said Mikey, sitting down on a front row chair. He balanced his clipboard on his left leg, which he rested horizontally on his right leg, revealing at the ankle an expanse of deeply hideous multicoloured sock. I glanced over at Sam on her side of the stage, and snorted as I saw her put her fingers in her mouth in a gagging action. I had to admit she was growing on me.

"Right, I think I've got it," Mikey announced, standing up. "Deena, what about we get you to interact with Elise at this point?"

Deena had been sitting next to Sean – we were doing the party scene – but now skipped to the front of the stage, obviously pleased at being singled out by Mikey for a more important role.

"Of course, that leaves us with a bit of a gap . . . Um, Chris, do you think you could take over Deena's part, please?"

I hadn't expected to hear my name, and must have looked exactly like a startled bunny caught in a car's headlights.

"OK, Chris?"

"Yes!" I squeaked.

"Right, people," said Mikey, slapping his palms together, "we haven't got much time before the caretaker comes and chucks us out. So let's mark our way through this scene nice and speedy, so we can get wrapped up."

So that's how I suddenly found myself being

spun through the air by Sean Miller, as per the script. And then, as he lowered me down till my feet touched the floor, I felt his lips gently, lightly, brush mine, as per my wildest dreams.

Chapter 9

I'd managed to concentrate on precisely nothing for the whole week.

It probably didn't help that Laurie wasn't around to talk stuff over with – she'd fallen *way* behind with an art project after getting all wrapped up in her dad and the new baby. She'd just sussed out that her A levels were only a month away, and was starting to freak out a bit. My teachers were getting pretty hyper about the exams too, but me . . . all I could think about was Sean and that kiss. And what the hell it meant. Now, finally it was Saturday, and Laurie had promised to give me her undivided attention – as well as some party therapy.

The house was huge. Like, *enormous.*

"What does your mate's dad do to have a

place this size?" I asked Laurie, trying to crunch my way as quietly as possible across the vast gravel driveway.

"Oh, it's her mum, actually – she's some big flash lawyer. Her dad just plays golf all day, I think," Laurie answered. "They're both pretty snobby, but Katrina's all right. She was one of the few people who didn't treat me like an untouchable when Dad ran off with Yvonne. Anyway, I wouldn't hear a bad word said against her – not when she's been kind enough to have a party and invite us." Laurie grinned and pressed the doorbell.

"Invite *you*, you mean. She doesn't know me from anyone. She'll probably have her guard dogs escort me off the premises!"

The heavy wooden door swung open, and a smiley girl in a shiny minidress and bobbing bobbed haircut squealed hello.

"Katrina," Laurie said, turning to me, "this is my friend Chris."

"Hi! Well, come on in – there are loads of people here already," she beamed, ushering us into an expensively carpeted hallway. This girl's folks were just going to love having the usual party debris stomped into their pricey old Axminster! I thought to myself.

"Laurie, be a darling and chuck your jackets up in the guest room at the top of the stairs, would you? You know where it is, don't you? I'll show Chris round. Come on! This way!"

I trotted meekly behind Katrina, who reminded me of the jolly but firm woman who shepherded us around at Brownies.

"Sitting-room. . ." she said, breezing through a room with three fat four-seater sofas, already being lounged on by people I didn't recognize. Giant speakers on either side of the marble fire-place blasted out some kind of dance track I didn't recognize either.

"Dining-room. . ." We walked through a set of flung-open double doors into the connecting room, dominated by a long polished table. Beautiful wrought iron candelabra stood on top. Someone who looked slightly drunk was kneel-ing up on the table trying to light all the candles with a wobbly hand and a Zippo.

"Jake, scratch that table and I'll kill you. Get down *now*!"

The boy slithered sheepishly off the table. Yep, Katrina was definitely like my old Brown Owl.

"Right, the conservatory's through there," she said, pointing to what was obviously the most popular area to hang out so far. "Through that way is the kitchen if you want anything to drink – but use the plastic cups I've set out and not the glass ones in the cupboards, please. The down-stairs loo is through there too. If you get desperate there's another bathroom upstairs, but I'm trying to stop people from going up there.

Mummy said, 'Katkin, have a fabulous party, but if I find any stray souls crashed out in the upstairs rooms when we come back I'm going to be very cross indeed!'"

I nodded non-committally, trying not to let my mouth twitch into the laugh that was bubbling up inside. "Mummy"? I'd never heard anyone over the age of five call their mum that. And Katkin? How cutesy could you get? It almost made my own nickname sound cool by comparison. At least Conk was short and to the point (unlike the nose it was named after), and not some stupid babyish marshmallow of a name.

Laurie arrived at my side just as Brown Owl shot off to answer the door to more new arrivals.

"All right?" she asked.

"Yeah, fine. But I think Katrina could have saved herself a lot of effort if she just gave out photocopies of the floor plan and a set of rules to everyone who comes through the door."

We were in the kitchen, rooting around the fridge for Coke (for me – ever since the night of Laurie's birthday I couldn't face the idea of anything remotely alcoholic) when I heard a familiar laugh. Turning sharply, I looked through the hallway and into the dining-room. Sure enough, there was Lewis, cracking up at something or other, with – inevitably – Sean at his side. I could feel prickles of panic on the back of my neck.

"Laurie!" I hissed. "Sean's here! And Lewis!"

"Really? Where? Tell me and I'll look subtly."

"In the dining-room – Lewis's got fairish hair, and Sean's next to him with dark hair and a blue T-shirt." My throat was tight with nerves.

Laurie, bless her, did an excellent manoeuvre, turning from the fridge, gazing round into the dining-room, then picking up her bottle of beer from the kitchen table in one smooth non-obvious move.

"Come on, let's go and sit in the garden and work out how to handle this situation," she said, opening the back door and motioning me to follow her outside.

It was quite a warm night, and we sat on a white wrought iron bench, set a little way back from the conservatory. The reflection of the lights burning there didn't quite reach where we were sitting, so we could watch everyone inside while remaining incognito out there in the dark.

"So how do you feel?" Laurie asked.

How did I feel? How had I felt for the past week? Elated, excited, delirious, confused, mystified. Any of those would do.

Ever since that briefest of butterfly kisses last Sunday, I hadn't known what to think. The kiss itself was over in a microsecond. I don't think anyone else saw it: my hair had fallen forward as Sean lowered me to the floor, obscuring both our faces at the crucial – fleeting – moment. But straight away we were all bulldozing through the rest of the play at a speed of knots before we ran out of time, and our eyes didn't seem to meet again. As the caretaker waited patiently to lock up after us, I saw Sean and Lewis disappear out of the door. Would Sean be waiting outside for me, ready to explain what had happened? Keen to re-enact it at a slower pace? Desperate to ask me out? My heart was in my mouth as I stepped out into the late afternoon sunshine – but there was no sign of him.

I managed to ruin the next day by being in a tizz of anticipation before the usual drama group meeting. I got out of English late (Mrs Ellis couldn't make up her mind how many million essays to give us for homework), and had to run to Mikey's classroom. Breathless, I practically charged into Sean just inside the door – had he been hanging around on the lookout for me?

"Chris, I. . ." he began shyly, putting his hand on my arm. But that's as far as he got; Mikey interrupted with a forceful "C'mon! Let's start!" and Sean drifted off towards Lewis, glancing back at me with a wistful expression.

No boy had ever looked at me wistfully before. I couldn't wait for the end of the class – what would he say to me? The anticipation sent pitter-patters of palpitations across my chest. But ten minutes before we broke up, Sean asked to be excused – he had to leave early for some reason or other. I felt sick with disappointment as I watched him disappear out of the door. When would I get the chance to talk to him again?

Every day after that, I held my breath as I walked along the school corridors, ever hopeful of bumping into Sean. But as the week went on, and I'd had no sightings of him, I began to doubt the whole kiss thing had ever even happened.

"I feel sick," I moaned.

"That's understandable," said Laurie, brushing my hair away gently from one side of my face.

"I feel horrible," I whined.

"You look fantastic," she said, adjusting the choker she'd lent me. It was silver with a black onyx star dangling from it, and it did go great with my fail-safe spaghetti-strapped black vest and jeans. She'd done my make-up too – black liner along the top lashes, with nearly-black shadow dragged over it, to soften the edges. My bottom lashes were bare – not even mascara. It was a very old-French-movie-with-subtitles look. I loved it. Laurie looked great too; she was wearing a long dark-green shift dress with a tight white T-shirt underneath and kids' style white plimsolls. And even in the near-dark I could make out the sheen of her long red hair.

"I feel like I want to go home," I bleated.

"No way! Look, I'm sorry to tell you, but doing something and then acting like nothing's happened is a very common boy reaction.

Anyway, maybe he'll come over and talk to you about it tonight! It's perfect really, there's nothing like a party to loosen people up a bit."

I panicked when I saw her stand up.

"What we're going to do is go in and talk to some people I know, then you're very casually going to wave hi to Lewis and Sean, and then turn back to us and look like you're in the middle of a great conversation. Right?"

"Unghhhh. . ." I muttered, letting Laurie drag me reluctantly towards the conservatory door.

"Hi, Chris!" said Lewis, pushing past dancers in the packed room to appear by my side. "I didn't realize you'd be here tonight!"

"Well, same here! I mean with you! Both of you . . . er. . ." As choreographed by Laurie, I'd managed the casual wave thing quite success-fully – Lewis waved and grinned back, while Sean gave me a quick smile and a nod. What did that mean? But now the talking thing: I was losing it. Not 'cause of Lewis – I felt pretty com-fortable speaking to him now – but because I desperately wanted Sean to pop up beside him, and at the same time I *dreaded* Sean popping up beside him. . .

"Yeah, well, we just heard about it through a girl Sean knows at St Mary's."

Who did Sean know at St Mary's? Jealousy instantly burned in my chest. And where was he?

I couldn't be so rude as to look over Lewis's shoulder for him. But I was dying to.

"I'm here with my friend Laurie," I said, pointing over to where she was standing and at the same time grabbing a handful of Hula Hoops from a bowl on a small marble-topped table. "I'll introduce you in a minute."

"OK," said Lewis, staring at Laurie's profile. I knew it wasn't something I was into, but it didn't hurt being associated with a cool mate. "Listen, Chris, while we're talking surprise guest appearances, I just wondered if you'd seen that Faith arrived about ten minutes ago."

"What? Where?" All my shyness vanished instantly and I frantically scanned the crowded conservatory and the dining-room beyond.

"I dunno, I just saw her come in the front door with a few of her mates when I was coming out of the kitchen."

"How the hell did she know about this party? She doesn't know anyone at St Mary's!" I was practically yelling at poor Lewis, I was so angry. It was bad enough having Faith skulking around at home (OK, so she did live there), and potentially any corner at school, but having her invade my private life was just too much to bear. What stories would she try and tell Mum *this* time? Oh God!

"What's up?" said Laurie, probably anticipating some romantic disaster, seeing me talking to

Lewis and looking so upset.

"*She's* here," I practically whimpered.

"Who?" asked Laurie, confused.

"The wicked witch of the west," said Lewis.

"Oh, you mean *Faith*," Laurie nodded at him, knowingly.

"Laurie, that's it – I'm leaving. I've just got bad vibes about tonight."

Lewis and Laurie started in with protests. They were both being brilliant, and here I was, such a rotten mate I hadn't even bothered introducing them to each other properly. I didn't have the energy for niceties right at this point.

They persuaded me that I had to stay, so I took the easy way out and agreed, then said that I was going to the loo, secretly planning to nip upstairs afterwards, find my jacket and shoot off. I didn't want to mess up Laurie's night and make her feel like she had to leave too, but a house full of posh people I didn't know, a bloke who'd gone all weird on me, and the gloom I felt at knowing Faith was around just didn't bode well.

Who cared if it was Saturday night? Right at this point the thought of cuddling up on the old sofa in Rob's room with a corny late-night movie and a packet of tortilla chips sounded like absolute heaven.

Whoever was in the loo was taking for ever. I was on the point of heading off to find the bathroom upstairs (if Brown Owl hadn't cordoned it off already), when the door finally opened and out poured two giggling girls – Faith and her mate Emma.

"Oh, what an unexpected treat!" Faith said drily, her smile instantly gone and replaced with a stony expression. "What brings you here, Conk? Fed up of relying on middle-aged men and dodgy nightclubs for your social life?"

I tried to push past her into the loo, but she put out her arm and wouldn't let me through. Instead, I stared at the ground and tried to work out a response. All that came to my mind was to tell her that Mikey was only twenty-five, but that wasn't going to get me anywhere.

"I'm here with my mate. Leave me alone."

"Gee! This promises to be interesting."

"What do you mean?"

"Well, let's face it, your choice in friends isn't exactly sound, is it?" smirked Faith.

"There's nothing wrong with Laurie!"

"I wasn't talking about your hippy chick mate – it's just that I've heard you've been getting very chummy with the school's top slag."

For a second I was confused, then the realization of what she was getting at dawned on me; she was talking about Sam.

"There's nothing wrong with Sam!" I blurted out. It wasn't like I knew the girl all that well, but one thing I knew for sure – there was a lot more to her than her dodgy reputation.

"Oh, sure. Tell you what, let's have a little poll of everyone here — most of whom aren't even *at* our school — and see how many have heard about Sam the Slapper and her reputation. And you'd better be careful, Conk," she leant closer and I could smell the booze fumes on her breath, "people will start to see you the same way if you keep hanging out with her."

I looked into her grinning, spiteful face and wanted to scream. But before I did, a voice distracted me.

"Hi, Chris. You all right?"

All at once the anger slipped away and I felt myself turning into a pathetic pile of mush.

"Uh, yeah. . ." I mumbled in response to Sean, as I watched him squeeze past us from the kitchen, can of beer in hand, and head into the dining-room. Once again the Law of Fancying People had struck, where it's impossible to talk in anything like a normal way to the object of your desire.

Dragging my gaze away from his receding back, I turned to face Faith.

"Ahhh. . ." she said knowingly, her expression letting me know that she'd immediately sussed my feelings. She turned to Emma, saying, "C'mon, let's mingle," before leading the way towards the dining-room.

* * *

God knows how long I stayed in there, but it felt like sanctuary.

I sat on the loo for ages, my head resting against the cool marble tiles of the wall, trying to calm down. After that, I stood at the sink a while, letting the torrent of cold water run over my wrists and feeling the soothing watery rush slow my racing heartbeat. It wasn't till I heard hammering on the door and Laurie's voice that I finally dragged my wet hands over my face and through my hair and went to open the door.

"Chris! I was worried! Are you OK?" Behind her stood a queue of curious – and presumably desperate – people.

"Sorry," I said, shamefaced, to Laurie and anyone whose bladder I'd inconvenienced.

Once we were in the kitchen, I tried to explain what I thought Faith was up to, but it didn't sound so convincing when I put it into words.

"I don't think Faith's going to try to snog some guy in the year below her just to get at you. She wouldn't see that as a very cool move, would she? Don't forget that appearances matter to someone like her. Nah, she'll be after some of Katrina's brother's college mates. Trust me, Chris."

"I know, I know," I answered, starting to feel like I'd overreacted a little. "But everything's been spoiled now and I just want to go home. You don't have to come."

"Course I do," she said, giving me a hug. "Let's go get our jackets."

I pulled on my denim jacket in the darkened upstairs hall, while Laurie gave it "one for the road" as she said in the bathroom before we left for the long walk back home.

A breathless gasp made me jump. It's funny how the dark can do that – make you jump at sounds you wouldn't pay any attention to in the daytime. I pussyfooted my way along the corridor towards the source of the sound.

There it was again. How funny! Someone was obviously breaking Brown Owl's strictest rule and getting hot and bothered in one of the untouchable upstairs rooms. I couldn't resist peeking. But even before I'd pushed the door open enough to spy in, I knew who I'd find. He had her pressed against the window-sill, kissing her neck, their outlines illuminated by the light from the conservatory below.

"Faith, oh, Faith!" Sean practically groaned.

Chapter 10

The industrial-strength lino had seen plenty of scuffing feet over the years, and today I was dragging my feet so badly along the corridor that I was sure I'd leave grooves in it. The last thing I wanted to do was see that creep Sean in drama group. And I couldn't bear the way I wanted to see him so badly too.

"Brilliant, Chris! I was beginning to think you weren't going to make it. And we can't really afford anyone being off with only two weeks to go to the performance!" Mikey's big warm smile made me feel like crying for some reason. Anyone saying anything remotely kind to me at the moment might set me off.

I tried not to look at the rest of the group, as I shook off my blazer and stuffed it and my bag on to one of the last empty chairs at the side of the classroom. Over and over again in my head I kept praying that we'd just run through the end of the play and skip the party scene, saving me the agony of reliving that dreamlike kiss.

"I think we should just concentrate on the end of the play today, if that's all right with everyone," said Mikey. I could have kissed him. Figuratively speaking, of course.

During the last few scenes, I knew I didn't have to have that much contact with Sean; I just had to stand fairly close to him. It annoyed me when I felt myself shaking as I walked over to my position – no way did I want him to realize how much he'd upset me. Crossing my arms, I focused directly on Mikey and pretended to be engrossed by what he was saying. Still, I was aware of Sean's presence so close to me, like a subtle buzz of electricity, but I couldn't – wouldn't – make eye contact. What would his face have given away? Awkwardness? Apology? Regret? Probably none of those. I mean, it wasn't as if he even *knew* I knew about him and Faith – I'd closed the door silently on them before they'd even sussed that they'd been caught. And he certainly wouldn't be thinking about our fleeting kiss after his full-blown snog-a-thon with the glamorous Faith!

Of course, there *was* a chance that he knew I knew – if he'd been in touch with Faith since Saturday's party, I guessed. That was because

Faith went all out to let me know what had happened in her own special way, spending the whole of Sunday afternoon on the phone to her mates, boasting of her ability to "twist that be-sotted little git Sean around my finger". She made sure she spoke extra loud when I was passing, desperate to get a reaction. Having spotted her when she didn't realize it kind of spoiled her nasty little surprise, of course. It must have gutted her to watch me walk by with a blank face. She would have been hoping for buckets of tears at the very least.

So had she been in touch with Sean? She was so two-faced I could just imagine her purring down the phone at him two seconds after bad-mouthing him to her mates. I hadn't heard her talk to him, but I had spent chunks of the day round at Laurie's or up in Rob's room. It was at times like this I really missed Rob – he could have given me a boy's-eye view about what Sean was playing at (no prizes for guessing Faith's in-tentions), and if he couldn't, at least he'd have done his darnedest to make me laugh about it.

"Hey, Chris, how's it going?" said Sam as I pulled on my blazer at the end of rehearsal.

"Weird," I grumbled, not able to look her in the face, in case my eyes gave away the hurt I was feeling. "Faith got her claws into Sean at the party I went to on Saturday."

"Yeah, I heard – Lewis was moaning about it

to me earlier. Listen, we were both just wondering . . . do you fancy going for a coffee or a Coke or something?"

"I don't know what he's playing at, Chris, honest. I know he's supposed to be my best mate and everything, but I've got no idea where his head's at right now."

The three of us were sitting in a booth at the back of the overlit and practically empty Burger King on the High Street.

"So, what's the deal? Has he been hankering after Faith for ages or what?" I asked Lewis, stirring my lukewarm coffee frantically, even though the sugar must have dissolved ages ago. I felt kind of nervous talking to Lewis – and even Sam – about this. Did they think I was just shocked that Sean had snogged my hideous sister, or had either of them guessed that I had more than a passing interest in him myself?

"No . . . it's just that he said he was – well, *flattered* that she went after him. You know – older girl, really pretty, doesn't seem to go for any other boys at school. I mean, I tried to tell him she was trouble when I saw her flirting with him, but he just shrugged. And of course, by the time your sister got her claws in him he was drunk as a skunk, the stupid git!"

Lewis, bless him, had the decency to look truly embarrassed about what his mate had done.

"I can't believe Sean would be that shallow! And it's not like he doesn't know what a bitch she is – God, the whole school knows that! He knew how she treated you, and I thought we were all starting to become friends!" Sam shook her head in disbelief.

I suddenly decided to dive in with another piece of the puzzle and tell them about the kiss – after all, I still didn't have to admit my feelings for Sean.

"Lewis," I said quickly, before I bottled out, "did Sean tell you he kissed me at last Sunday's rehearsal? During the party scene?" Sam gave a little gasp, and Lewis nodded.

"Yeah, yeah, he did."

"Well? What did he say? It felt pretty weird to be kissed out of the blue and then . . . then just nothing."

"Didn't he talk to you afterwards?" Lewis looked genuinely surprised.

"He kind of started saying something to me at drama group on Monday, but then he shot off," I shrugged, hoping I was giving the impression of being just mildly perplexed rather than what I really felt – confused, upset and completely and utterly gutted.

"He told me he was going to talk to you."

"And say what?" My heart was hammering inside my chest.

Lewis was staring at the plastic stirrer he was

twiddling nervously between his fingers.

"Well, he said it was just a bit of a laugh, a spur of the moment thing. He was going to tell you next day that it had just been – y'know, a bit of fun."

"That's *it*?" said Sam, enraged.

I felt my eyes start to sting, and tried to blink away the tears before anyone noticed how miserable those words made me feel. At that moment, Lewis looked up straight into my face, his brown eyes fixed on mine searchingly.

"Look, Chris, if it makes you feel any better, I felt like punching him when he said that," he burst out, almost angrily. "I'm going to get another coffee. Anyone want one?"

So it was just like Laurie had said the day before when we'd talked the situation over in her calm, white room: some boys are just plain obnoxious. They give out all the signs that they're decent human beings, then they go and do whatever takes their fancy without having the decency to give their actions the tiniest bit of thought. I didn't want to believe it of Sean. He was too sweet, with his shy smiles and the way he hid his gorgeous face behind that flop of dark fringe. Until this conversation I'd been certain, no matter what Laurie said, that there was some kind of explanation for him behaving the way he did. No matter how much I'd strained my brain, I couldn't think what that explanation could possibly be, but I'd been sure there was one.

Right up until this point, when the horribly bright, blinding light of truth suddenly struck me in Burger King.

"I know you liked Sean ... a lot," Sam said quietly when Lewis disappeared off to the counter.

"How?" I asked, feeling those treacherous tears welling up again.

"Hey, I'm good at this stuff – I can always tell." Sam put her hand over mine. "And I also know how bad it feels to be mucked around."

Poor Sam! I thought, in the midst of my own misery. Everyone assumes she's this airhead who skips happily from one bloke to another, but there's obviously more going on there than anyone gives her credit for.

"Anyway," she smiled, giving my hand a squeeze, "even before all of this, I thought you were after the wrong boy."

I must have looked completely puzzled for a second. Sam laughed and nodded over to Lewis, who was weaving his way precariously back to the booth, three steaming coffees balanced between his hands.

"I mean *Lewis*, you idiot! He's lovely, he's funny, and he's mad about you!" she whispered, as he came closer. "Oh Lewis, I told you not to get me another coffee – I've got to go –" she glanced down at her watch and her eyebrows shot up in alarm – "right now, or I'll be late meeting Gavin!"

With a blow of a kiss at me and a flirty wave of the fingers a few centimetres from Lewis's nose, she was gone. Lewis and I were suddenly alone, and in the light of what Sam had said, I felt ridiculously self-conscious.

"I really am sorry that Sean's been such a pillock, Chris," he said, staring into his cup.

"It's not your fault, Lewis! There's nothing you could have done."

"Yeah, but he's my mate, and I . . . I think of you as a mate now too." Again, he lifted his eyes to meet mine. "And it makes me feel terrible if he's messed you about in any way."

I felt the warm glow of flattery wash over me. It was a nice feeling after a particularly weird week in the emotional department.

"Chris, can I ask you something?"

"Yeah, of course!" I said, wondering what was coming next.

"Do you fancy going out sometime? Maybe to the movies or something?"

Oh boy! This felt strange. Lewis was great, much nicer than most boys I'd known – smart, funny, kind, thoughtful, and (according to Sam) smitten with me. A natural blast of excitement zapped through me, but . . . but . . . I just couldn't think of him that way. I should say thanks, but no – I only wanted us to be friends.

Was I being stupid? Not giving him a chance? Then an image pushed its way into my head: a darkened room, two figures illuminated by the bedroom window, one gasping while the other muttered a name. . .

"I'd love that," I said, and watched Lewis's face light up.

Chapter 11

I had yet another cop-out postcard in my hand for Beth (*So much has been happening: I promise I'll write properly soon!*) and was aiming for the postbox outside the gate by the science block when I heard sobbing. Not some big, dramatic, look-at-me histrionics, but heart-wrenching gulped sobs, the breaths in between practically hiccuping on top of one another, as if the person was trying very hard not to be heard and to get hold of themselves.

Whoever was so upset was obviously just round the corner, and I paused mid-step, wondering whether I should intrude or not. But there was no sound of voices, so whoever this was, they were on their own. That did it for me. At least if I offered to help I'd feel better, even if they told me to bog off.

"Sam!" I said with surprise as I stepped forward and caught sight of her, huddled on the steps of the fire-escape.

As I hurried towards her, she looked up at me, her trademark flickable hair tangled and damp where she'd tried to push it off her tear-drenched face. Her eyes were bloodshot from crying and smears of mascara were easing their way down her puffy cheeks.

"Oh, Sam!" I said, plonking myself down by her side and putting my arm around her. "What's wrong?"

"Gav-Gavin just finished with me!" she managed to get out before her face once again crumpled into tears.

"God, I'm so sorry," I said, full of surprise and amazement. Surprise that Sam was so upset at losing an arrogant, unreliable git like Gavin, and amazement that she hadn't seen it coming – Gavin had been mouthing off so much about her round school lately that it was obvious his feelings weren't exactly sincere. Hadn't she cottoned on to that in the way he treated her, even if she didn't know what he was saying about her behind her back?

"How did he put it?" I couldn't help asking, then immediately felt guilty for being so nosy. "You don't have to tell me if you don't feel like talking about it."

"No, it's – it's OK. He, um, he came up to me

in the dinner hall queue just now and said he – he wanted a word," she hiccuped, then stopped to blow her nose on the paper tissue I'd dug out of my pocket for her. It was a bit dusty and scrunched up and I had an awful feeling I'd used it already, but Sam was past caring. "And he took me out here and, and just said he wasn't into it any more. . ."

"Was that it? No more explanation than that?"

"Oh yes, there was more," she sniffed bitterly. "He said that since I wouldn't go all the way with him, there wasn't any point carrying on."

"What – you mean *sex*?"

"Yeah, that's what it came down to. I really cared about him, really loved him, y'know, Chris?" she looked at me with reddened eyes brimming with tears. "And I thought he felt the same about me. Then it got to 'If you loved me you'd sleep with me,' and now it's 'So you won't, so get lost.' "

I felt out of my depth, like I'd missed a vital part of the plot somewhere along the line. Gavin had chucked Sam because she *wouldn't* have sex with him? But wasn't that why he went out with her in the first place? Wasn't that why any of her boyfriends went out with her? I felt like a traitor thinking these thoughts about someone who'd started to become a mate, but it was common knowledge round school what Sam was like!

"I can't believe I got it so wrong, Chris. I really thought this time I'd found someone who loved me for *me*."

I nodded numbly, still trying to work out if I'd picked her up wrong in some way.

"It's like this every time I go out with a boy. I think, here's someone special, someone I can trust, then it all starts happening again." Sam dabbed at her eyes, starting to sound a little calmer, but more flat and resigned. "The dreaded 's' word comes up, and when I say no, they're off like a shot."

I couldn't think of a thing to say, and I guess Sam clicked what was going through my mind.

"I know what everyone says about me, Chris – I'm not an idiot. But I'm not what they think."

"Oh," was all I managed to say.

"Chris, I'm a virgin."

I hated the journey home on the bus compared to the mornings – it was always mobbed and it was practically impossible to get any seat, never mind my spot at the top. Today I was squashed on the back seat on the bottom deck, in between some giggling primary school kids and a middle-aged woman with enough Tesco's bags to feed a family of nineteen.

It occurred to me that I hadn't seen the Mad Old Bus Pass Lady for a while. I wondered what had happened to her; I hoped she was all right.

Then my mind skipped to the fact that Dad was due home very soon, which I prayed would cheer Mum up – she was still pretty moody. Next, I started thinking about what I should wear for my date with Lewis that night, and wondered why I felt strangely unsettled at the idea of going out with him. Basically, my mind was working overtime, hopping from one subject to another in a pathetic attempt not to think about what Sam had told me.

It wasn't the shock of finding out that the entire school and a particular strain of horrible boys who fancied their chances had got her so terribly, unfairly wrong; no, it was more than that. And it wasn't the sad truth that I'd come to realize about Sam, that she – sensitive and lovely girl that she was – was so desperate for affection that she couldn't help herself going out with wrong boy after wrong boy, ever hopeful that one of them would be her big love. It was hurtful too to think that somewhere down the line she went out with one show-off liar who started the rumours about her, and it spread on like Chinese whispers, with the creeps she dated keeping up the pretence of having a wild time with her just to keep face in front of their moronic mates.

Yep, all that was depressing, but what was more depressing was when Sam asked me if I'd heard anything about Sean and Faith. I'd been driving myself mad all week thinking of the two of them going out together, so I was more than keen to hear what was going on.

"It's all round school, you know. Apparently, someone found them in bed together at that party. I just thought you should know."

I was floored. I just hadn't expected that particular bolt out of the blue. Now, sitting on the bus with noise and bustle all round me, I tried to force myself to face the horrible fact that Faith had slept with Sean. She had sussed out that I liked him and systematically gone after him at the party, out of sheer spite. But getting off with him was one thing; what really scared me was she had gone as far as having sex with him. Surely going to that extreme must show how much she really, *really* hated me.

Lewis held up a selection of CDs in a fan shape in front of me.

"Go on, you choose!"

I smiled and tried to look enthusiastic, but it was hard to change an essentially rubbish day into anything remotely pleasant, no matter how well intentioned the other person was.

"That one," I answered, pointing to an album that I vaguely remembered seeing in Rob's collection at home.

We were sitting on the floor in Lewis's room, which was tidier than I'd have expected, with paraphernalia restricted mostly to one big cork pinboard and fairly minimal mess in the dirty clothes/old music papers/empty cans of Coke department. It was done up pretty well too – nice pale green walls, with a brilliant original fireplace against one wall. He'd got a collection of weird and wonderful candles all along the mantelpiece – those sort of swirly patterned pyramids you get in hippy gift shops. Lewis's room wasn't about to be featured in any of those home-decorating telly programmes, but it wasn't half bad. If I hadn't been feeling so miserable, I'd have been quite impressed.

Our original plans for the evening had gone wrong (oh what a surprise, on this great day of days). The movie we tried to get into was sold out, our second choice had started half an hour earlier, and every food place that we could afford on the High Street was packed out. In the end we came back to Lewis's house which, being on the far side of the park, was much closer to the High Street than mine. I was relieved that my house wasn't really an option – the thought of exposing him to my formerly fabulous and now trimmed-down, less-than-welcoming family would have given me a migraine.

"I could get us a couple of my dad's lagers, if you fancy – he won't mind," Lewis offered, looking at me with big puppy dog eyes. Oh God! I didn't want him to be like this with me – I wanted to see the usual cheeky grin. I just wanted him as a mate, a good mate, but then I'd obviously changed all that by agreeing to go out with him on a date, hadn't I?

"Not for me, Lewis. I'm OK."

"Cool. I won't bother either. I'll stick out this main light," he said scrambling to his feet, "and put some candles on – that's always better."

Oh *God*!

We talked about lots of stuff: favourite movies, favourite music, favourite comedians. We agreed on most things, and if we'd been having this conversation along with some of the others during drama rehearsals it would have been brilliant. But there was just the two of us, and the air of expectation made our words feel somehow awkward. We didn't mention anything about Sean and Faith, even though we'd sat discussing it along with Sam only a few days before. Now it felt like an unspoken rule that it was too close to home, too sensitive to bring out into the open.

Suddenly we were silent, with only the music in the background filling in the space where our voices had been. I was aware of Lewis, who was sitting only a metre away, moving closer.

"Chris. . ." he said softly, cupping one side of my face with his hand, then running it back through my hair, pausing at the back of my neck. Gently, he pulled me towards him.

In contrast to this slow-motion action, my mind was racing. I should break away now, before we kissed and spoiled everything. What would it be like to kiss Sean instead? Did Sean know Lewis and I were together tonight? Would he be jealous? How could Faith have slept with Sean? Had she slept with anyone else? She hadn't been out with that many people that I knew of. Were they seeing each other? I'd hardly seen anything of her all week. What was it like to have sex with someone? It couldn't be a big deal – not if Faith could do it like that at the drop of a hat. . .

Then his lips were on mine, soft and warm. I shouldn't be doing this. I don't want to be doing this. I let him kiss me for a long time, felt the faintest touch of his tongue on my lips. He began to bend me back towards the floor, and I moved with him. He ran his hands up and down my back, across my waist, only just touching the bare skin that was showing where my shirt had ridden up. I don't think he would have gone any further than this; he wasn't a Gavin or a – damn him! – Sean. He would have slowed down or stopped at the slightest indication from me, I knew he would.

But my mind was ablaze. I was angry, furious for being a fool, for falling for the wrong person, for being a mug and being stood on by Faith. I wanted something for myself. I'd show them.

Next thing I knew I was pulling Lewis towards me, grabbing a handful of his fair hair in my hand and kissing him hard, almost desperately.

He gasped; coming up for air, I could see the surprise in his eyes. I pushed my hands under his T-shirt, my fingers sensing the sweat on his back, and pulled him down towards me for another kiss before he could say anything.

"Lewis, do you or your friend want a coffee? I've just put the kettle on," came his mother's muffled voice from the other side of the bedroom door. We stopped, frozen, the madness of the moment broken.

I had to get out of there.

I headed home through the park, half-running in the twilight and worried that the gate at the other side would be locked before I got there. I know it's pretty stupid to do something like that on your own at night, but I wasn't really thinking straight, and all I wanted was to get back home as fast as possible.

It was completely dark as I jogged breathlessly towards the house, and the bright lights blazing from the windows looked warm and welcoming. Even though I'd had pretty mixed feelings about home lately, I felt a rush of comfort as I approached – as soon as I got in I was going to kiss Mum (touch wood, Faith would be out), run a big bath, then hole myself up in front of the telly in Rob's room with furball Gus for comfort until I could get a chance to talk this all out with Laurie in the morning. She'd tell me what to do. She'd make sense of it all.

My head was bursting for some tranquillity, but as soon as my key was in the door, I realized I wasn't going to find it here. In the hallway stood Mum, clutching the phone, shouting above the din of the blaring TV. She hardly took any notice of me.

"No, Jim *Woods*, not Jim Cook! No, I don't know what shift he's on! Yes, it *is* an emergency. Look, can't you put out a call for him? It's his wife! Yes, yes, I'll wait!"

She sounded hysterical. What on earth was wrong? But the wave of panic I felt rushing over me instantly subsided when I spotted the well-worn rucksack propped up against the stairs.

"Hi!" mouthed Rob, silently, giving me a sheepish wave from the kitchen.

Chapter 12

"Well, Rob, I think that went very well."

Rob let out a groan as he stumbled sleepily towards one of the chairs round the kitchen table. I'd been up since about eight o'clock (sacrilege on a normal Saturday morning), hoping I'd have time to get him to myself for a while before Mum got up. I guessed she'd sleep on for a while this morning – she'd been so wound up and upset the night before, I'd made her take a couple of sleeping pills when she finally made a move to go to bed. I reckoned if she got a good night's sleep she'd be slightly more reasonable this morning. Faith didn't even know Rob was back – I'd heard her stomping in around 1a.m., long after we'd all flopped exhausted into bed.

"Enough of your sarcasm, madam. Any

chance of some tea?" he grinned at me, before letting rip with a big yawn.

I found him his favourite mug, shoved at the back of the cupboard, and stuck on a couple of bits of toast for him as the kettle boiled. It was lovely to have Rob back, even if it was just for the weekend, and even if he was here only to tell us he'd definitely made up his mind to do the charity work.

"What the hell was all that about last night, Chris?" Rob asked me, his hair sticking up madly in all directions, courtesy of Pillow Hair Designs. "I mean, I expected her to be upset, but I didn't think she'd go ballistic like that, screaming at me and trying to get hold of Dad at work and everything. You'd think I'd told her I was taking time out of university to be a serial killer, the way she reacted!"

"Yeah, thank goodness she didn't manage to get hold of Dad! She'd have freaked him right out the way she was carrying on." I plonked his tea and toast down in front of him. "To be honest, she's been a bit weird lately, Rob. Like really overreacting to stuff, or being kind of distant, away in her own little world."

"What do you mean?" he said, looking less sleepy and more concerned.

"I don't know, it's hard to explain. She's just not herself. We never really chat any more or have a laugh like we used to. And she's blown up at me quite a few times – she's never done that before."

"Yeah? Why didn't you tell me?"

I felt a rumble of irritation, not something I usually felt with Rob.

"Like when? You haven't been home since Christmas!"

"You could have phoned me—"

"I can never get through to that damn place you stay!"

"Well, you could have written!" He was kind of right, but not being very fair either.

"So could you, Rob. I mean, I love all your postcards, but Mum's been really upset that you never phone or write to her."

"Hey, Chris, do you realize how hard it's been for me at uni?" He looked at me angrily, pushing his plate to one side. "I'm trying to survive on as little money as possible so I don't end up with huge debts or having to sponge off Mum and Dad; I'm struggling to keep up with the course-work—"

"But I bet you've still got time and money to go to the student bar plenty of times in the week!" I was sniping – I knew I was – but I was angry too and couldn't help it.

"What's that supposed to mean?"

"I mean you could have stayed in the *occasional* night to write Mum a letter, or spared a couple of quid every now and then to have a

144

good chat with her on the phone. Hell, all you needed to have was a 10p – she'd have called you right back!"

"So Mum being like this is *my* fault, is it, Chris? Well, thanks – thanks very much. Just chuck another weight on my shoulders, why don't you?"

I put my head in my hands and tried not to cry. This wasn't what I wanted. Rob was my best mate – closer than Beth had ever been, closer than Laurie could be. We'd never had an argument in our lives (only jokey ones about which video to watch), and here we were laying into one another.

"Rob, listen," I said, looking up at him. "I'm not saying anything like that. But stuff's happened in my life too, you know. And you don't know what it's been like the last few months, with you and Dad both gone. Mum's changed, and I can't get through to her, and Faith's just out of control! I feel like the only sane person in the house, and I don't feel like I'll be that for much longer, the way things are going!"

"OK, calm down, Chris," said Rob, reaching over and taking my hand in his. The old Rob was back, but I still felt rocked by his lack of understanding. "What do you think is going on with Mum?"

"I don't know. I'm just worried it might be something to do with Dad – I mean, she's always grumpy with him when he calls, and yet she's always moaning when he doesn't. I'm scared about them splitting up, Rob. I don't know it's that for sure, but—"

"What's going on?"

We both turned around, Rob still holding my hand, and looked at Faith standing in the kitchen doorway.

"What are *you* doing home?"

"Well, it's good to see you too, Faith," Rob half-smiled at her. "I'm just home to tell Mum I'm going away for a couple of years. I'm going to do charity work abroad."

"Oh," said Faith flatly, her face giving nothing away. "And what were you saying about Mum and Dad?"

"Chris was just saying how Mum's been edgy recently, since Dad's been away."

Faith looked at me like she could kill me – why, I couldn't figure out, but then nothing about her surprised me these days – and suddenly turned and stomped back upstairs.

"Nice to have chatted with you, Faith," muttered Rob as she left. "So, she's been giving you a rough time then, has she?"

"You wouldn't believe the half of it!" I sighed.

"Right, save those stories – I'm going for a shower, then you can come and tell your Uncle Rob all about it."

On my own in the quiet of the kitchen, I

realized that this latest family drama had its up side – at least it had taken my mind of the mess I'd made of my date with Lewis.

Rob was still in the shower and I was in my room trying to brush the tangles out of my hair when I heard the phone ring. Mum answered it – she was awake and downstairs obviously, although I hadn't heard her get up. I couldn't make out what she was saying, but I heard her voice move from a normal pitch to something more angry in seconds. I was riveted to the spot when I heard the phone being slammed down, followed by the sound of sobbing. Oh God, what now?

Rob and I rushed out into the upstairs hall at the same time – he was rubbing at his wet hair with a towel – and looked at each other in sympathy and panic before we trundled down the stairs. As I took the first step, I heard a creak from the top of the next flight of stairs and looked up at Faith's bedroom door. Our eyes met for a second before she slammed the door shut. I carried on downstairs, ready to face whatever.

Mum was in the kitchen, sitting with her head in her hands, crying so much her back was heaving with the effort. She looked for a split-second like a five-year-old in mid-tantrum, but I knew this was far more serious.

"What's wrong, Mum?" I asked, rushing to one side of her as Rob hurried to the other.

"He doesn't care!" she mumbled tearfully.

"Who doesn't, Mum?" asked Rob.

"Your father! He doesn't care enough to come home, and he doesn't care enough that you – his own son – is going!"

I looked at Rob over the top of Mum's head and shrugged.

"What do you mean, Mum? Are you saying he isn't coming home this week like he planned?" My heart was racing. Was he leaving her – us?

"No. Leave cancelled, he said. Another two or three weeks at least, he said," she practically spat out, her voice full of bitterness.

"So his company has cancelled his leave?" I asked, trying to piece this story together. Now it was starting to make more sense – my pounding heart was slowing down to its normal speed as I realized it was all out of Dad's control, not through any choice on his part.

"Yes, but at a time like this, I can't understand why he doesn't just pack it all in and come home anyway."

"A time like what, Mum? I'm not some big drama to be solved!" Rob seemed furious. "I don't want Dad rushing back here to sort me out like some little kid who's done something wrong! I'm an adult, Mum, and I'm doing something really worthwhile, not telling you I've done an armed robbery or something!"

"How could you, Rob! How could you!" Mum sobbed, sounding hysterical again.

"That's it," said Rob, standing up, his face white and taut. "I'm out of here."

As he strode off upstairs, grabbing his rucksack as he went, I thought about running after him, but Mum seemed too upset to be left alone. Anyway, I was too angry, too disappointed in him. I felt scared. I didn't know what the hell was going on with my mum, but *I* wasn't about to run off and leave her.

I heard the door slam a few minutes later and knew he had left.

"Mum, I don't understand what's happening. Please talk to me." I stroked her hair, like she used to do to me when I felt bad as a kid. She lifted her head, and sat up straight, immediately looking more like my mum and less like this strange, distant person she'd become in the last twelve hours.

"I don't know, Chris, I just don't know myself," she said, giving me a little shaky smile.

Then she talked and talked – stuff that I knew a little bit about already, like her hating Rob and Dad being away so much, all jumbled up with other things I didn't realize. For instance, I knew the woman she worked with was off on maternity leave, but I hadn't understood that meant Mum had been landed with all her work as well as her own. Then she began to speak about Gran.

There were plenty of times when I thought of Gran and missed her – just being in Rob's room, surrounded by the furniture he'd chosen from her flat when she died, brought back memories of her – but it had never occurred to me that my mum had lost her own mum.

"I know I'm a grown woman, Chris, and I should have managed to cope with her dying and everything, but I haven't. I miss her all the time." She was speaking more calmly now, which made me feel marginally less uptight myself. "And the trouble is, I don't think Faith's over it yet either, but I just don't have the energy to sort myself out, never mind her."

"Faith?" I said, startled. I hadn't really thought she'd crop up in this conversation.

"Chris, I know what she's been like recently, but you've just got to be a little patient with her. You remember how close she was to Gran?" I nodded numbly. "Well, I think her death hit Faith really badly, but you know what she's like – she'll never give away what she's feeling. I think she's just angry at everybody and everything. I just wish I could help her, but right now, I don't know how to."

"Is that why you've been covering for her all the time? Why you're always taking her side?" I said, a sudden realization dawning on me.

"Have I been doing that, Chris?" Mum looked at me, surprise in her eyes. "Well, yes, I suppose

150

I have. It's just that you and Rob are so – so confident and self-reliant. Faith – well, I think she's a lot more vulnerable than any of us realize."

I didn't know what to say to that. I'd been so battered and bruised emotionally by Faith recently that it was hard to feel any sympathy, but in a way, Mum's words made sense. Like I say, Faith had never been an angel, but if I traced it back, then yes, she had got worse in the last year, which fitted in with what Mum had been saying. And it was true that she was close to Gran – she was the only one Faith didn't act up with.

"Sorry, Chris," said Mum, sounding more like her old self. "Have I upset you prattling on like this?"

"Oh, no, Mum!" I didn't quite understand why all this had made her act the way she had, but it felt good to know what was going through her head. "I actually thought – well, that maybe you and Dad were going to split up—"

"Oh Chris! No! That's the last thing that would ever happen!" Her eyes were filling with tears again – I had to do something fast before she lost it again.

"Mum, I'm going to run you a big, hot bath with some of those aromatherapy oils I got for Christmas," I said brightly, "and you're going to lie in it for at least an hour and be completely lazy. OK?"

There! I didn't know if that would be remotely helpful, but it seemed like a grown-up thing to do. Mum smiled at me appreciatively.

This was weird. I was the youngest in the family, yet suddenly I felt I was the one holding everything together.

Once Mum was in the bath, I unplugged the phone from the hall downstairs and brought it up to Rob's room. There was a phone point in there (Rob had toyed with getting an extension, but when he thought how much extra talking and therefore phone bill contributions he'd have to make, he soon changed his mind), so I knew I could have a bit of privacy.

"Laurie? It's me, Chris."

"Chris! I was just about to call you! So, how did the date go?"

"Oh, just about as bad as it could possibly go. I really messed things up."

"How?"

"I – I don't know, Laurie. One minute I was think-ing how much I didn't fancy Lewis, and how much I wanted to get out of there – not that the poor guy was being anything but nice to me – and the next . . . well, I just let things get out of hand."

"Like?"

"Like, I kind of came on to him."

"Chris, what were you playing at?"

"I found something out yesterday about Faith

and Sean – they were caught in bed at the party last week."

"No!"

"I think I just flipped out last night, you know?"

"Poor baby. Come right round now and let's talk about it."

"I can't, Laurie – I've got another problem."

After listening to me for a minute, she told me to hang on. I heard mumbles and footsteps in the background and was surprised to find Megan on the other end of the line. She made me talk her through the whole Mum scenario.

"Chris, dear, I think all that's wrong with your mum is that she's bottled up a whole lot of things and she's basically suffering from something like nervous exhaustion. I felt and acted quite like her when Laurie's dad and I were parting. Now, what you should do is call up and make an appointment for her with the doctor. In the meantime, I bet she'll feel miles better for having finally opened up and started speaking about how she's feeling. Just you keep listening, Chris, and being supportive; you're the best medicine your mum's got right now."

Her words were comforting, and I felt a warm glow at the idea of being the one Mum could count on, but at the same time, the weight of the responsibility was quite crushing.

"If you like, I could maybe pop round over the weekend and have a chat with her."

"Er . . . no, that's all right, thanks." I didn't think Mum would relish the idea of her first meeting with Megan being some big heart-to-heart because of me blabbing my mouth off.

I had just put the phone down from speaking to Megan and was wondering where I could find the health centre number when the door was flung open.

"You little bitch!"

I was thrown. Had Faith been eavesdropping? Did she think I was out of order talking to someone else about Mum? Her face was contorted with rage.

"What?"

"I've been sitting trying to work it out, and it just hit me right this second—"

"What are you on about?" She was freaking me out.

"Don't come the innocent! I heard some interesting gossip last night – about myself. And I've been wondering who'd want to spread such a vicious little lie about me. It was *you*, wasn't it?"

"What lie?"

"Don't give me that! You're just a jealous little cow because Sean fancied me and not you!"

Rob's CDs rattled in their rack as Faith slammed the bedroom door shut.

Today was turning out to be even worse than yesterday. And it was still only half-past ten in the morning.

Chapter 13

"Oi!" I called after Faith.

I'd had it. It was time to stand up for myself. If there was one good thing to come out of the traumas of the last couple of days, it was that suddenly I didn't give a damn any more. I'd stopped being afraid of Faith.

Thundering up the stairs after her, I barged into the attic bedroom. She'd flopped backwards on to the bed, her arms crossed defensively across her chest, staring up at the ceiling.

"Get out!"

"Faith, if you're talking about the stuff about you and Sean at the party, then yeah, I've heard all about that, but—"

"Well, it's not exactly hard to have heard about it since you're the one going around telling everyone!" Faith pushed herself up on the bed, looking like some kind of big cat in pounce position.

"I did *not* tell everyone!"

"Oh, yeah? Then who else would have been interested enough to start off a rumour like that? Nobody else gives a damn about my love life!"

"Hey! You don't know or care about someone like Sam Reid, but you're pretty quick to believe and pass on any gossip you hear about her!"

"That's not the same at all. Sam's a tart and I'm not."

"Well, I'm sorry to disappoint you, but I know for a fact that Sam is *not* a tart. And as far as who started any rumours, anyone at that party could have done it. You're such a cow that there's probably a waiting list of people who'd love an excuse to bad-mouth you!"

"What are you saying!"

"Forget what *I'm* saying; what are *you* trying to tell me – that it's not true about you and Sean? You didn't sleep with him?"

"Of course I didn't sleep with the little creep! I just can't believe people think I would have!"

"Aren't you Miss High and Mighty!" I spat out sarcastically. "You're outraged that people could swallow the story that you had sex with Sean Miller, when of course all you did was go after a guy you didn't fancy in the least *and* snog his face off for the pure and simple reason that you

156

wanted to piss me off. How could people get you *so* wrong!"

Faith – her face pink with anger – seemed to be struggling for something to say, but no words got past her lips.

"See? You can't even come up with an answer to that, can you? You've had everything your way for so long, you can't handle it when something happens that's out of your control!"

I'd obviously hit a raw nerve.

"Get out! Leave me alone!"

I nearly did turn and leave her to stew – after all, I think it was fair to say I could retire victoriously, having won my first ever battle with her. But then again, this *was* the first time I'd ever got the upper hand where Faith was concerned, so it seemed a shame to give up when the going was so good.

"No. Tell me why you did it – why you got off with Sean. Let's hear your grown-up, well-considered adult reason."

"I don't have to explain anything to you."

"No, of course you don't. You can just go round for months – no, make that *years* – giving me hell, but you don't need to justify that. It's what any girl would do for her sister. It's such a joy to have you as a member of the family, it really is!"

I would have carried on, but then I wasn't such a bitch as Faith. She was surprising me by not fighting back, by not lunging at me and scratching my eyes out. She was staring wordlessly at the carpet. I hunkered down, trying to look up into her face.

"Say something! What are you thinking?"

There was a long pause before she spoke, and when she did it was very quietly, hardly more than a murmur.

"I haven't got anyone."

"What do you mean?"

"All my mates have been giving me real grief – calling me names, calling me a slag and everything. I couldn't work out why till I made Emma tell me last night."

I realized the implications for Faith; in her little gang of vipers she was top dog until – as it tends to go with girls like these – they found a chink in her armour and that was that. They smelled blood and they were out for the kill. It was all just entertainment for them. It was hard to feel sorry for Faith though – she'd played by exactly the same rules for long enough.

"They're a bunch of cows, Faith. Everyone in school knows that." And thinks of you in exactly the same way, I thought wryly. "So what if they're acting that way? Dump them!"

At that point she whipped her gaze away from the carpet and met my eyes.

"Oh, yeah – and hang out with who exactly?"

I was stumped. Who else would touch Faith

with a bargepole? Her friendship skills weren't exactly finely honed.

"And none of *you* give a damn about me."

Again I was stumped. It was true that as far as me and Rob went, Faith's innermost thoughts and feelings weren't something we considered too often, but then she'd hardly made herself lovable over the years. Did she mean our parents too? Surely she couldn't!

"What are you on about? Mum and Dad—"

"Dad's always away, and he's so busy trying to make up to everyone when he finally gets home that he never really listens to what I'm saying, and Mum's gone weird and is only interested in him lately."

"Faith, that's not really fair. I just had a talk with her and—"

"Oh, isn't that cosy? You and Mum and your cosy little chats! She never just sits and chats to me." Probably because you never give her the chance, I thought. "And then there's you and Rob, always ganging up on me!"

"Faith! That's *so* not true! Me and Rob—"

"'Me and Rob! Me and Rob!'" she mimicked, pulling a face and rolling her eyes upwards. "God, you two make me sick! Always cackling away at your pathetic in-jokes! You think you're so smart!"

I groaned. Here we go! I thought. The jealousy thing about me and Rob.

159

"With you two it's all giggle, giggle, giggle, then, 'Oh, look! Faith's come into the room. Let's go silent and stare at her.'"

As I was about to open my mouth and let rip about how ridiculous she was being, a flicker of an image popped into my mind – how it must feel to be standing on the other side of the door to Rob's room, hearing us laughing together at some ancient Pink Panther movie, or chattering away about some new group or other. . .

"Don't say it doesn't happen, because it does," she continued without pausing. "Look at the two of you this morning – yakking away, then as soon as I ask what you're talking about, you clam up!"

"No Faith, you've got it wrong. I was just kind of guessing at what was wrong with Mum – it was nothing worth repeating!"

"I heard you though," she said softly, looking at me with something close to panic in her eyes. "Do you really think they could be splitting up? 'Cause I couldn't stand that!"

From my crouching position on the floor, I twisted myself round and scooted across the few metres of carpet on my bum to the edge of the bed where she was sitting.

"No, no! That was one of the things Mum was talking to me about. That's absolutely *not* going to happen – she just hasn't been feeling great lately, that's all." Faith looked so relieved it was almost touching. Almost. I still wasn't quite ready to shake the hand of my torturer.

"What's up with her?"

"Oh, I think it's just a whole load of things that have got her down – work, Dad and Rob being away . . . and she *did* say that she's not really got over Gran's death yet. She – well, she said she thought you hadn't either."

I primed myself for the usual forceful, derisory denials, but all Faith muttered was, "Did Mum say that?"

Leaning up against the bottom of the bed, I noticed for the first time that Faith's room was full of bits and bobs from Gran's house: on her dresser were a few of the empty but beautiful glass perfume bottles Gran had let us handle so gently; the copper vase that sat in her hall was over on the window-sill, complete with the paper-thin branches of honesty that Gran had always kept in it for as long as any of us could remember; and on the wall was the framed photo of Gran and a smiling two-year-old Faith on her knee that used to sit on top of her telly. I don't know why it surprised me, but it did. Of course, I'd known that Rob got some of her furniture for his room, and Mum had her big clock in the living-room, but it hadn't occurred to me where all Gran's smaller stuff had gone.

"Do you still miss Gran a lot, then?" I asked tentatively, not looking too closely at Faith in case she was upset. I suspected she'd rather punch me than let me see her crying.

"Of course. She was the only one who really rooted for me, y'know? You always had Rob to go to. . ."

I knew what she meant, I guessed. For a second or two we sat in silence, until a timid knock at the door interrupted our reverie. Mum peeked tentatively into the room, looking sweetly young all wrapped up in her big white towelling dressing-gown. Her face was a picture at the sight of her two daughters doing something other than fighting.

"Oh, I thought I heard shouting when I was in the bath."

"No, Mum, everything's fine," I said firmly. "Isn't it, Faith?"

I was going to be hideously late for this afternoon's rehearsal. Mikey had asked us all to come down to the community centre where the show was happening so that we could get a feel for the stage we'd actually be performing on, along with about ten other youth groups who were acting, singing, dancing and doing whatever else for the entertainment of the whoever paid their money and showed up on the following Thursday. Luckily (I guess), so much had been going on in my life that I hadn't the energy to feel nervous about it.

Still pulling my jacket on as I yanked the gate shut behind me, I nearly jumped out of my skin when a hand descended over mine on the latch.

"It's only me, your idiot brother," said Rob, looking extremely sheepish. "Kind of made a mess of that earlier, didn't I?"

I nodded.

"I got as far as the train station and realized what a drongo I was. Sorry. I'd better get in there and sort it out, hadn't I?"

"It's mostly sorted," I told him, with a certain amount of pride, "but I'm sure Mum would be glad to see you anyway."

Back in the world outside home, things weren't going quite as painlessly as I'd hoped. All through the afternoon Lewis wouldn't look at me, no matter how much I tried – nervously – to catch his eye. And who could blame him? I'd acted so bizarrely the previous night he probably didn't know what to think. Which was fair enough – neither did I. I desperately wanted to make it up to him, to be (just) friends again, but I didn't think I could possibly get over my embarrassment enough to make a move if he wasn't responding. And anyway, I reckoned I'd used up my entire goodwill quota for the year in the space of a morning.

By contrast, I had the strangest feeling that Sean was trying to get my attention. Not that I was about to acknowledge him in any way. In fact, it was a real relief to find out that all we had time for was a quick technical run-through this afternoon, which got me off having to have any proper contact with him. I had one dress rehearsal on Monday after school, followed by the show on Thursday, after which I'd never have to go near him again.

We'd nosed around backstage, practised our entrances and bows, and now the technicians were trying out some spotlights for Marianne and Elise. Sam used the lull as an opportunity to motion me over to the wings for a quick gossip.

"How did last night go?" she whispered.

"Don't ask!"

"Uh-oh! That sounds bad."

"I'll fill you in later." There was no way I was going to start telling her tales when Lewis was only about three metres away from us.

"Still, what's going on with Sean?" she hissed. "He keeps giving you meaningful looks."

"Well, he can look all he wants – I don't want anything to do with him. And," I leaned closer to make sure we weren't overheard, "it turns out that stuff about Faith and Sean sleeping together isn't true."

"That's brilliant!" she squealed at me, a little too loudly.

I didn't get her drift, which must have been

obvious from my expression.

"Think about it, Chris – that means he's not as bad as you thought. He only made the mistake of kissing her, so why don't you just let it go? You still like him, don't you?"

Was I being too hard on him? After all, it wasn't as if we were going out together. I hadn't even let him know how I felt about him. But then he knew what Faith was like, and how she treated me. If he was my friend, along with Lewis and Sam, should he have gone off with her like that? And what about that unexplained kiss? The rush of confusion I felt was interrupted by Mikey.

"OK, folks, I think our time's up. Thanks for coming, and I'll see you all on Monday." He was wearing a cool grey V-neck top with his jeans today, instead of his usual naff heavy metal weekend wardrobe. Could Megan be having some influence over him in the style department, I wondered?

He turned to me. "Chris," he said, "could you do me a favour and give our details to one of the organizers up at the back?"

Taking the typed A4 sheets out of his hand, I walked up to the table full of mostly middle-aged ladies, who were dealing with other performers and scribbling details furiously. As I got closer, one white-haired elderly lady began to look increasingly familiar to me.

"Hello," I said tentatlively, handing over our

details to her. "You used to take the same bus as me in the mornings."

"Did I, dear? That's nice," said the Mad Old Bus Pass Lady.

"Um, I haven't seen you for a while though," I waffled on, not really sure why I was carrying on a conversation with someone who obviously didn't know who on earth I was.

"Yes, well, I've moved you see, dear. To the sheltered housing unit round the corner. That's what this concert's raising money for."

"Ah!" I said, stupidly. I was mortified to realize that it hadn't even crossed my mind to ask what the whole shebang was in aid of. And now I was struggling for some way to get out of this conversation. "Still, it keeps you busy, then?" I said limply.

"Oh, yes! Got to get everything sorted. That's what's important, isn't it, dear?"

She was only saying something to be polite, but I knew there and then that the Mad Old Bus Pass Lady was right. It was important to get things sorted. I'd seen that this morning with Mum and Faith, and now it was time to straighten things out with Lewis, if he'd let me. And if that went well, then who knows, maybe I could start softening up about Sean. . .

I got my chance straight away. Lewis was in the foyer on his own, struggling to get a can of Irn Bru out of a reluctant vending machine.

"Lewis?" I said tentatively, unsure how he'd respond to me. When he did turn round, his expression was hard to read; it was as if he didn't know whether I was going to kick him or kiss him.

"Chris, I – I'm sorry about last night," he burst out, eyes like saucers.

"No, no!" I yelped, horrified that he felt *he* had to do the apologizing. "Lewis, it's me that's sorry! I got everything muddled up, I guess. Everything's been mad for me lately, and I – well, I got things wrong."

"Oh. OK. Fine. I understand," he nodded, then stopped. "Actually, I haven't a clue what you're on about."

We looked at each other for a second then both started giggling. I know it was mostly just nerves, but it was nice to break through that awkward atmosphere that had been hanging around all afternoon.

"It's kind of hard to explain, Lewis. The only way I can put it is that I didn't know what I wanted. I think."

"And do you know what you want now?" he asked me shyly, hopefully.

"I know I want us to be friends. It just doesn't feel quite right to think of us – y'know, in a romantic way." I hated to see the way he looked, so dejected and disappointed.

"That's a shame," he said, looking down and

scuffing at the lino with the toe of his trainer. "I'd kind of hoped. . . Well, you know what I hoped." I felt such a rat that I kept quiet for a moment. "Still, at least we're talking, still friends and everything. I was beginning to feel pretty lonely there."

"How come?" I asked him, confused.

"Haven't you noticed? Sean and me aren't exactly big buddies at this point." I hadn't noticed, but that was because I'd been so wrapped up in my own dramas that other people's dilemmas had passed me by.

"But why?"

"You know that whole thing about him and Faith? The rumours that have been going around about them?"

"Yes, but they're not true!"

"Oh, I know *that*. Trouble is, Sean's getting quite a buzz from everyone thinking it *is* true. Like earlier this week, some of the lads were asking him about it, and he just played along. Afterwards, I really tore into him. It was just such a pathetic thing to do."

So! Sean Miller had just found himself struck off my goodwill list.

Chapter 14

It had been a funny old week. Mum, me and Faith had all tiptoed round one another, none of us really referring to what had gone on or been said on Saturday morning, but it was still quite nice, like all of us were trying that little bit harder. And while I wasn't saying anything of any importance out loud, plenty was going on in my head. I guessed that was pretty much the same for both of them.

I took Rob next door to meet Laurie on Sunday afternoon, which gave me a chance to fill him in on the events of the previous day. He felt gutted that Mum wasn't well, and guilt-ridden for having stormed out on her. But if that took him by surprise, the stuff I told him about Faith blew him away. It came as a shock to him – as it had to me when she told me – to think that Faith had always felt we pushed her out, which was the complete opposite of what we'd always thought. It was good to have Laurie there to talk it through with too, since she'd been aware how miserable Faith had been making me feel the last few months. She pointed out that Faith's the sort of person who never likes to have a weak spot, and reckoned that she'd been building up her sadness and anger over Gran's death for so long inside that it all just spilled out into the bitterness that we were all too familiar with. She made a lot of sense. Of course, I knew that Faith wasn't going to turn into a sweet fluffy bunny overnight – she'd always been hard to live with and probably always would be – but it helped to get a handle on what was going on with her.

I think Rob was really impressed by how smart Laurie was. I mean, he liked Beth and everything, but I think he wasn't quite expecting me to have found a friend who was more likely to analyse feelings than giggle about them. God, that sounds mean, doesn't it? In fact, I think the guilt about comparing Laurie and Beth is why I made a concerted effort to start my letter to Beth again that night, after Rob had packed up and headed back to university. But then I realized there was a new Jane Austen adaptation on the telly and never quite got round to doing it after all. Oops!

There was a bit of an atmosphere at school through the week too – but unlike home, it wasn't a particularly pleasant one. In between dodging the whispers still going round about Sean and Faith and the teachers getting edgy about the exams looming after the approaching half-term, there weren't many laughs to be had. Everybody in the drama group was getting excited and nervy about Thursday's show, but again, there was a problem – loads of the teachers were a bit iffy about us all getting time off in the afternoon to get ready for it. What did they think? We'd all fail our exams because we missed two stupid hours of lessons a month beforehand?

Come the evening of the show, another problem arose. The make-up girls for one of the other groups hadn't turned up, and because they had to have animal faces painted on (they were doing a dance to that 'Wim-a-way' song from *The Lion King* – and no, it was actually *worse* than you can imagine), Mikey kindly offered the services of our make-up bods, since their need was greater than ours.

I've always been rubbish at putting on anything more than lipgloss, and that, combined with nerves made me freeze in front of the bulb-framed mirror. Luckily, Sam came to my rescue, managing to apply some eyeshadow for me, despite her hand trembling ever so slightly.

"Hey," she laughed, "you realize we'll all be getting offered jobs on *EastEnders* after this!"

"Yeah, in the staff canteen," I muttered darkly.

171

* * *

"Before we went on I felt really sick, and now I'm just kind of – well, dizzy!"

"That's normal, Sam; it's only adrenaline playing games with you. Even actors who've been doing the rounds for years can feel like that." Mikey was beaming, obviously chuffed that we'd got through our piece with no hitches. "How was it for you, Chris?"

"It all went so fast! I remember being aware of a sea of faces when we first came on, and then blam! We were taking a bow!" I replied, trying hard to make sense of the show we'd just done. My knees still felt pretty wobbly, but it seemed a bit wimpy to bring that up. I mean, it wasn't as if I'd had that much to do. I was in awe of Marianne and Elise for having held the play together so well. Facing a whole audience, I think I'd have freaked out and forgotten every one of my lines, if I'd been them.

"I thought the play was brilliant, really funny," beamed Laurie. Beside her, Megan smiled and nodded in agreement.

"Yes, it was very good, darling. It's a pity Dad wasn't back in time to be here." Mum stretched across the row of seats that separated us and gave me a little hug. All through the hall, this scene was being repeated: no one in the audience had been in a hurry to leave when the evening's entertainment had finished, because practically everyone had friends and family who'd performed and who they wanted to congratulate.

"So, Faith, any comment?" I grinned at her.

"Yeah. See that old dear who was selling pro- grammes? Didn't she used to get on the bus in the mornings?"

"Uh-huh," I nodded. I guessed that was as much as I was going to get out of her. Expecting any praise or comments about the show was probably hoping for too much; I was just amazed that she'd come at all.

"Listen, I'd better go and do the rounds with everyone else. Catch up with you later!" said Mikey, heading off to chat to some of the others from our group.

"God, I forgot to pick up my jacket!" I suddenly realized, looking around me frantic- ally, as if it would appear by magic. "I must have left it in the changing room. I'll be back in a minute – don't leave without me!"

I bounded off up the stairs to the stage and pushed aside the heavy velvet curtain. Stepping through the darkened wings, my heart did a quick somersault: I'd not only made my stage début (a small but perfectly formed part), but practically all the most important people in the world to me were gathered together out at the front. Just for little old me. Even – amazingly enough – Faith. Who'd have thought it?

* * *

I bent down, reaching out to drag my jacket from where it had fallen on to the dusty floor underneath the make-up counter. A sudden scuffle from somewhere behind me in the changing room made me realize I wasn't alone.

"Hi, Chris!" said Sean shyly, his dark fringe flopping over his forehead. It was the first time I'd consciously noticed his habit, the way he always blinked his long-lashed eyes. It made him look like Bambi. It annoyed me.

"Hi!" I answered warily. I didn't want to be by myself with Sean. It had been uncomfortable enough having to hold hands with him during the play, and I'd focused on a point somewhere above his head when he'd had to whirl me round.

"Chris, I wanted to talk to you."

Is that right? I thought, but stayed quiet. I didn't feel like demonstrating any friendliness towards him.

"I just wondered if you wanted to go out with me sometime."

This I hadn't quite expected. This time, it was surprise that kept my mouth shut.

"I've always liked you, Chris. You must have known that."

"Why? Why should I have known that?" I burst out. He didn't seem to notice the irritation in my voice.

"Well, I mean, that time during rehearsal. . .

When we kissed. . ." he said, his long eyelashes fluttering appealingly at me. Was I meant to melt or something? I couldn't be bothered with this any more.

"Sean, I've always wanted to ask, why exactly *did* you kiss me then?" The sarcasm in my voice shot right over the top of his head, and he blinked at me, all innocence.

"It . . . er . . . it was just one of those things. It just felt the right thing to do at the time."

"OK, Sean, so let's see," I said wearily. "First you kiss me because it 'felt right', then you tell Lewis that you're going to talk to me and tell me it was just a bit of a joke – except you never quite get around to it, 'cause obviously it's something that's just not all that important to you. But now you're telling me you always liked me?"

"It just took me a while to sort out how I felt, Chris, that's all. Seeing you the last couple of weeks, and feeling like you weren't talking to me for some reason, I just, I. . ."

As he flapped around for words, it suddenly occurred to me that *that's* what Sean liked in girls – playing hard to get, which is what he obviously thought I was doing. It made sense of why he went off with Faith at the party; having the most aloof girl in school as a love trophy suited him down to the ground. Speaking of Faith, it was time to see him squirm his way out of this one.

"Right, let's suppose I believe that you really,

really like me. So, where does Faith fit into all this? If you like me so much, why did you end up snogging her at the party?"

His face drained of colour.

"Jesus, you can't hold that against me, Chris! It wasn't my fault! I just had too many beers and she came on to me!"

Looking into his wide-open eyes, I realized that he genuinely thought this was a perfectly acceptable explanation. I'd had such a lucky escape. This guy was a wolf in sheep's clothing. A crocodile with Bambi's eyelashes. He was going to make some unlucky girl a really terrible husband one day.

"Get lost, Sean," I said, turning and walking away from him.

"Faith was right! She said that night that you were an uptight, snobby little bitch!" he shouted after me.

Oh boy! Sean was making it ridiculously easy to get over him. Faith, of course, would probably always make it difficult to like her. But I'd give it a go.

Epilogue

The video that Faith's just flung at me isn't in the best condition – it looks like it's done the rounds at Blockbuster. Still, it's another small miracle in the new and fascinating world of getting to know and understand Faith. There was a time when I never thought I'd see it again, when it mysteriously "vanished" from the pile in Rob's room (my room officially, as from today, of course).

Walking over to the cupboard where I've tidied the tapes away (in alphabetical order, I'll have you know), I consider a few other not-inconsiderable miracles concerning Faith, like her coming through to watch the odd soppy movie with me (I realized that these did the trick for her, not comedy stuff); and sitting beside me on the bus to school from time to time. On the bus, she never says that much, just flicks through her magazines and bitches about the models and pop stars in them, but it's OK. I know that it's not all newborn sisterly love that makes her do it — since the Sean rumours, she fell out big-time with all her cronies, so I'm her only option. I think she gets a bit lonely without them, but she's been pretty busy with A levels (and Dad being home), so it's all right. And in September she's starting a course in occupational therapy at college (she managed to swap from the business course she was originally going to do), so she's bound to make new, improved friends there.

Inevitably, Faith more or less sailed through her exams, while I struggled my way through my GCSEs. The last one was English on Thursday (I think it went OK). To be honest, the exams weren't so bad to deal with; having Dad home for a few weeks really helped. He's been trying to make us laugh whenever he sees that we've got bogged down by them (me more than Faith, naturally), and, of course, Mum has just been in her element. She did go to the doctor in the end, which helped in as much as it proved Megan's theory about what was wrong with her; but once Dad knew, he went all out to help her, even making her start applying for better jobs. And he's promised her he'll only stay out in Indonesia for another six months, then look for something closer to home, which is brilliant for all of us.

Mum's fine about Rob now – not exactly thrilled that he's going away, but handling it. Just as well; he's off in three weeks to teach English in India. He's pretty sure he did OK in his first-year exams, and that'll make it easier to take up his course again when his time overseas finishes. Laurie and I might go and visit him next summer, if we can save, beg or borrow the money.

It's funny that just as Laurie and I became friends almost instantly, Laurie and Rob became an item pretty much the minute I introduced them that weekend he came home to break the news about going away. He wrote to her after that (a whole proper letter!) and they kept up a correspondence for the next few weeks until he came home last weekend. They've been out every night since. OK, so I'm a little bit jealous, but since their time together is limited, I can't really object. And considering my two favourite people have got together – well, that's pretty nice, I guess.

Speaking of favourite people, my Second Division of favourites has undergone a bit of a shake-up recently. Drama group stopped after the show – study time and exams took over, and it's not starting up again till after summer – but Lewis and I managed to meet a few times for a coffee. It was great to see him – I really hope we're going to stay friends and not let it slip. We were both a bit disappointed in Sam, though – we kept asking her along and she always let us down. Finally, she came and met us last week, using the exams as her excuse for her previous no-shows, but eventually she told us the truth. Basically, she was kind of embarrassed to see us both – and to tell us that she was seeing Sean. I felt bad for her – neither of us hid our shock very well. Lewis hadn't seen Sean at all over the weeks except in exam rooms, and I just couldn't believe Sam would go out with him after everything she knew about him.

"I know what you're thinking, Chris, but he's lovely deep down," she said to me apologetically as she was leaving. "And he really does care about me. . ."

Poor Sam! She still can't give up her pursuit of The Wrong Guy. But still, she's too good a mate to let go of now. I've told her to stop being stupid, and that we should make the effort to see each other in the summer holidays and not let our friendship slide. Of course, I've got one stipulation – I want to see her on her own, i.e. without Sean. Although, as Lewis says, God knows how long that little star-struck romance is going to last anyway!

Speaking of relationships – and that reminds, me, I'd better stop faffing around and get ready for the barbecue soon – another goodie is Mikey and Megan. Laurie says they're "making it official", i.e. Mikey's giving up his tenancy in the attic room and moving into the master bedroom with Megan. Laurie's really cool about it; she thinks they're brilliant for one another. Of course that now leaves a vacancy in the household, which is being filled at the start of the next term by a first-year drama student that Mikey knows of. He's apparently very sweet and funny, and Laurie (who's met him already) says that I'll have to help her look after him, especially if her college work keeps her too busy. I think I'll quite look forward to that.

"Hey, Conk! I forgot to tell you something!" Faith yells at me from her room. I get up out of the creaky chair and walk to the door.

"What?" I shout back up the attic stairs at her.

"The Mad Old Bus Pass Lady said hi!"

Faith has just started working weekends at the sheltered housing unit – as a care assistant doing the general dogsbody stuff – and she seems to be loving it, which is just as well, since she's going to be doing it all summer. Already she's had some great stories about our favourite old dear: her efforts to try and organize all the other residents to make up a line-dancing team, and how she still has her shopping trolley, filled, as Faith's discovered, with a never-ending supply of library books. So that's where she was going every morning!

"Tell her hi from me!" I yell.

Heading back into my room, inspiration suddenly strikes. I walk downstairs to the phone, trying not to tread on a snoozing Gus on the way. At the foot of the stairs, I unplug the phone and trot back up to my room. After rigging up the receiver to the output, I sit back down at the desk and idly watch the movement in the garden next door as I dial.

"Directory Enquiries, which name, please?" says the man's voice at the other end. Scribbling down the number he gives me on the edge of my English jotter, I scrunch up the half-started, half-hearted letter in my other hand and chuck it in the bin. It's about time I did what I should have done months ago if I'd had the sense.

The ringing tone burrs in my ear and I feel a flutter of anticipation as I wait for it to be answered. Just then, I notice Laurie in next door's garden, looking up at me and doing some strange pantomime actions. Rob's behind her, laughing. She's nodding her head dramatically to one side, and mouthing something at me. I push myself out of the chair and lean across the desk for a better view. On the patch of grass closest to the house, I can see Mikey flipping burgers on the barbecue, and next to him Megan is sitting on the conservatory steps, a glass of red wine in her hand, chatting to a young guy in black jeans and a pale blue T-shirt. His hair is dark and flops down to his shoulders, hiding his face from my view. I look back at Laurie and realize what she's mouthing: "That's him! That's him!"

The phone is burring on its fourth ring – it's bound to be answered any second. I'm in a quandary: hang on and catch up on months' worth of news with my long-lost best friend? Or go down and be hospitable to the soon-to-be new tenant next door? I clatter the phone down and glance around frantically for the trainers I kicked off earlier.

Catch you later, Beth!

Look out for other Confessions in this
revealing series

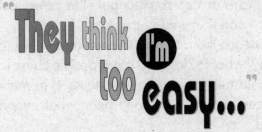

"They think I'm too easy..."

At break, I finally saw it – well, one of them. A notice taped to the wall just outside our class-room said, in straggly black felt tip, RACHEL KELLY IS A SLAG. SHE'S SLEPT WITH THE FOLLOWING BOYS. A list of boys' names followed. It included Sim, Lloyd, Paul and even mentioned the school caretaker, Mr Barlow.

I ripped it down, my face flaming. But there was another, larger one outside the gym, featur-ing a caricature of me wearing stockings, suspenders and a bra. An even worse one was outside the boys' toilets. CALL RACHEL FOR A GOOD TIME, it proclaimed, and then gave my phone number.

I was devastated. All I wanted to do was hide away from the human race. I raced off to the loo, locked myself into a cubicle and burst into tears.

Kirsty and Mary came after me.

"Rachel! Rachel, are you all right? Come out!" Kirsty kept calling.

"No, I'm not coming out. I'm never coming out. I can't!" I wailed tragically.

I heard them talking to each other. They didn't know what to do. Then other people came in and I could hear myself being discussed in muttering voices, though I couldn't hear what everybody said.

When I heard somebody mention fetching one of the teachers, I knew the time had come to emerge. Kirsty and Mary were still there.

"I just want to go home. I never want to set foot in here again," I sobbed.

Mary put an arm round me. She was being so kind, considering what a disgusting slag I was supposed to be. "Splash your face with cold water, it'll make you feel better," she suggested in her practical way.

I took her advice and did feel a bit better, though only physically.

"How can I carry on today, knowing everyone in the school's seen those notices?" I wailed.

"I'm sure they haven't all seen them," Mary said.

"It's not true! I'm not a slag!" I insisted, but my protest sounded half-hearted, even to my ears, because all at once I felt terribly guilty. After all, I'd slept with two boys in two months, and had gone a long way with a third. That was pretty dreadful of me.

It was so unfair, though, I thought miserably. If a boy slept with lots of girls, his mates envied his success and thought of him as some kind of hero. But if a girl did it, she was a tart. What had happened to equality of the sexes?

It took every ounce of my courage to walk out of the toilets and face the school. Even though the notices outside the gym and the boys' toilets had been taken down, there might be others elsewhere which I hadn't seen. It was obvious to me who the culprits were – those boys who had seen Paul and me half undressed in the doorway the previous night. They might have been watching us for some time, for all I knew.

As I walked down the corridors towards my classroom, I tried to keep looking straight ahead. I didn't want to make eye contact with anybody. Mary and Kirsty were still with me. We'd always been quite good friends, but suddenly I felt they were really good ones, and I'd never noticed. Where was Lori in my hour of need? She was supposed to be my best friend. I would have thought that, if anyone had stuck by me and tried to comfort me, it would have been her.

Outside the physics lab, I suddenly spotted another notice and felt sick. SLAGGY KELLY HAS

GREAT TITS, it proclaimed, and below the words was a crude drawing of naked breasts. Mary ripped it down for me, crumpled it into a ball and shoved it into her bag, while Kirsty gave my shoulders a squeeze.

"They're not worth bothering about. They're scum, the people who did this," she assured me.

I knew they were, but it didn't make me feel any better.

I was still red-eyed at dinnertime and terrified of bumping into any of the boys. All I wanted to do was get right away from school, but I couldn't. I was forced to stay there for the rest of the afternoon, as I had a really important class in which our French teacher was going to go through our translations of Verlaine.

My eyes scanned the walls as I walked towards the classroom, to see if I could spot any more of the nightmare notices. There weren't any, thank goodness. Presumably, the person who'd put them up had been too busy to do any more, or else my persecution had ended.